HUES

7 DIFFERENT COLORS

SABARINATHAN KULANDAIVELU

ISBN 979-888521318-9

Thirukural 784:

நகுதற் பொருட்டன்று நட்டல் மிகுதிக்கண்
மேற்சென்று இடித்தற் பொருட்டு.

Nakudhar Poruttandru Nattal Mikudhikkan
Mersenaru Itiththar Poruttu

-Thiruvalluvar

"Vibing together is not only the best fellowship thing; It’s great aspect is refining your thoughts when you are misguided"

Contents

Foreword

Inspirations

Dr. Deepa Ranganathan

(Author of **Unearthing your Emotional Intelligence**)

This book is extracted from the vibrant moments of my life packed with Joy, Fear, Struggles, Happiness, Guilt, Pride, Sacrifice, hope and the smile of feminine hues!!

Preface

I am Sabarinathan Kulandaivelu, an MBA graduate revolving in a routine robotic job life. I am a kind of student who focuses more on extra-curricular activities rather than as studious one. Since from my school days, I usually built scripts for AD-ZAP, stage drama, and sometimes even for getting permission for my illegal night outs.

The colors for this painting was stolen in 2017, at the time of fun filled trip to Wayanad with my dearest friends and referring to all my memories, fun, thrill, and overwhelming imaginations gathered from the trip are used as pillar to build the remaining story. After many reviews over that time, I concluded with a final version and kept as highly confidential file. Later, I have settled in a job life. In 2021, during the COVID-19 pandemic issue, I started to utilize the time with my Editors, by considering the script again and again by reframing the memories of my past life. I prepared **Hues** book with the help of my friend that used to be a well read as well as bed time story tool.

Thank you...

Happy Reading!

Sabarinathan Kulandaivelu
E-mail: sabaritheflickr@gmail.com
Insta ID:@sabaritheflickr

Acknowledgements

Sincere Thanks to
Sruthi Krishna Kumar
Dhinesh Sridhar
Vignesh Balasubramaniam
Prasanna Murali
Gayathri Rajkumar
Gokila Srikumar
&
Dr. Deepa Ranganathan
This book is an epitome of my inspired knowledge fused with the Locutions of Editors, **Ms. Srinithi Jawahar** and **Mx. Yashika Sruthi**
I dedicated this book to my Amma, Appa, my biggie-
Mr.Santhunu Raja Kulandaivelu
andmy overseas reviewer-**Ima Sivaprasath**
Thank you Readers !

Prologue

"If Friendship is your weakest point then you are the strongest person in the world"

-Abraham Lincoln

The entire world revolves with the presence of number of species; each distinct in its own way. Among all the living beings exist a holistic, pure and sometimes vulnerable creature named Humans. These humans are emotionally bonded with one pertaining to race, religion, community, work place, relationships and sometimes due to unexplainable factors. Such a factor that unites humans in spite of all the diversification; which establishes a noteworthy bond, gives more and takes less, dumps the disputes with an embrace, constitutes non-verbal deliverance of regret and gratitude, ensures the preservation of humanity; is the unique unification named FRIENDSHIP.

The story portrays the emotional connectivity of seven different lives. These seven people are brought up with mismatching identity and never intersecting lifestyles. They joined hands together in their under graduation and took forward the bonding over the years with the memories of all shades of emotions.

The crazy bunch of five IT professionals and two MBA grads maintain a daily contact via whatsapp and have a mandatory weekly once video call. The absence in these virtual gatherings would lead in the posting of an obituary poster on their FB walls followed by a special interrogation which is pure hell. There are committed and single candidates among the squad, yet it's the committed ones who remain present in these gatherings sincerely.

This squad is the Hues of this story; each associated with a shade related with their personalities. Water cannot be directly formed in a vacuum filled with Hydrogen and oxygen; it needs a spark in the vacuum. Similarly the exhilarating journey begins with a spark from one of the shades.

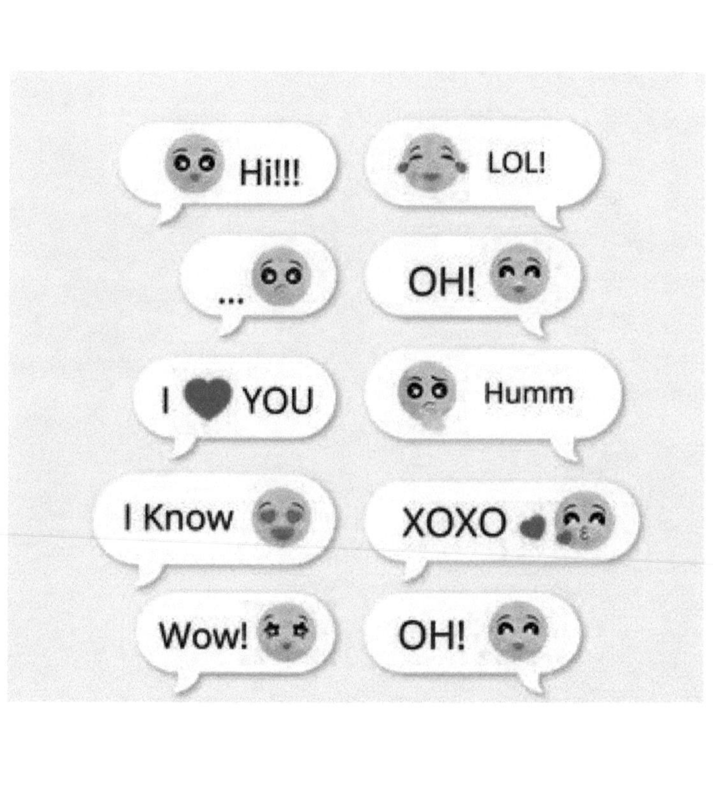
Hi!!!
LOL!
...
OH!
I YOU
Humm
I Know
XOXO
Wow!
OH!

CHAPTER I

Symbolize

Orange

(Bright, Optimistic & Uplifting)

Samyuktha, A millennial with a pretty face, and her kindness attitude makes her more beautiful; stood numbed in her college corridor located in Chennai. She felt that things are done once and for all and there is no restart button. Vidya, Samyuktha's best buddy and the only good companion in her college held Samyuktha's shoulder and made her to relax in a chair nearby.

"*Samyuktha, you need to be strong!*" said Vidya

Samyuktha gave no response and Vidya shook her to bring her back to senses. Samyuktha whispered "*What am I supposed to do Vidya?*"

Vidya replied, "*Why can't you go to your hometown and stay with....*"

"*Stay with...?*"

Vidya on realizing her folly said, "*Sorry Munchkin!*" Samyuktha's mother passed away when she was a child.

Finally a drop of tear rolled down on her pinkish cheeks. Suddenly Samyuktha's mobile rang and she handed it over to Vidya wanting not to talk. Vidya picked up the call. "*Hello Ma'am we are calling from GBI bank!*" Vidya with her agitated base voice said, "*Ah! Fuck!*"

Vidya cut the call and saw the wallpaper of her mobile. A pretty looking girl of medium height adorned in a classy look of orange one-shoulder dress with a tie-up waist had her arms wrapped around Ayesha, in the midst of her other hues. She has never seen Samyuktha's faceglow with such excitement.

Vidya turned towards her" *I want this Samyuktha back, My Samyuktha*".

" *Those days were priceless, with these giggles*".

It dawned upon her that she wants to be around them now. She got her mobile, openedWhatsapp and tapped on thehues group named **Gryffindor**.

Vidya smiled and patted Samyuktha. "*Go somewhere ; anywhere with your crazy bunch and come back to me soon*".

"*Vidya, I can assure you. These people will format my corrupted hard disk memories*", said Samyuktha and sent a text in the group.

"Trip...?"-04:00 PM

Green

(Determined, Jealous&Materialistic)

Among the skyscrapers in the RMZ Infinity tech park, Bangalore stood a start-up IT workspace buzzing with young minds struggling to get the code. Among them rose a tall, fair, straight haired, beardless, handsome guy with a perfectly maintained BMI. "*Guys!Bazinga !I sorted out the issues. I hope this weekend will be a stress free one*".

Everyone in the office screamed "*Kudos Michael!*" and went on to verify the answer. Michael,an Ameba shaped techie who flirts with women using his tech savvy spells and his voice is more mesmerizing than his idea; after having respondedto his team mates queries opened his draw and took out hisbrand new one plus. On catching sight of the green color dot notification he opened the whatsapp and read the text received in Gryffindor group. He smirked before replying to the text.

"Seriously..?" -4:03PM

Samyuktha"Why not?"- 4:04PM

Michael "I'm in. What about the remaining jerks?"- 4:05PM

Samyuktha "I can't even wait for their replies. I'll catch up with the girls & you go for our boys"- 4:07PM

Michael "Done Crazy Frog"-4:08PM

Samyuktha" Shut Up!"-4:08PM

Without a minute delay Michael opened the phone icon. Two contacts topped the frequent calls list and he called the same - Yash and Lenin who always stood for Micheal through his hardships. The line went ringing on and on and just when he was about to cut the call, the voice thundered from the other end, "*Dude!*" It is Lenin- a tall, arrogant, look-alike-giant ambivert photographer, who doesn't fit into the outlook of an MBA grad still pursued the management degree.

"*Why is there such delay in picking the call?*" Micheal questionned like a possessive girlfriend.

"*Sorry dude! I was riding on my bike*", he said teary-eyed, trying to override his emotions.

Michael ignored his apologizes and said" *Okay Listen! We are going for a trip*"

"*We?*"

"*Yes! You, me, Scarlett Johansson and your favorite Monica Belluci. Contented?*"

Lenin muted his phone to wipe out his tears and answered "*Dude! That's awesome!*"

Michael smiled "*Ass-a-whole I am going to kill you. I am mentioning our gang*"

With joy sending ripples across his face he asked, "*When? Where? Did everyone agree?*"

"*Keep up your spirit, Hippi. I have just begun with you. I will check out with the rest and get back to you*" status was updated from Michael.

"*Will he accept?*"

Michael with a freaky face exclaimed "*Fuck... dunno man. Let's hope for the best!*"

Suddenly, a mail popped on his system monitor asking him to perform the demo for which he sorted out the issue.

"*Dude! I have to go now. Catch you tonight*" Michael cut the call and clicked on the Start button to perform the application.

System started to compile and began its process. At the finishing stage of 98% it blinked an error with a RED color caution message.

"*Fuck Weekend!*"

Red

(Warm, Strong & Emotionally intense)

In a part of Tamilnadu where the Western Ghats ends, is a magnificent city named Coimbatore with a moderate temperature throughout the year. On a warm forenoon, Lenin, a Bodyguard structured MBA graduate who tattoted star in right arm, an arrogrant mindset, and an uncontrollable freak; was seated beside Amal, a frank and fitness freak, for the Emotional Intelligence class in the B-school. Lenin went on stalking Haya in spite of the class proceedings.

Amal whispered "*Bro! She doesn't give a damn about you. Why are you doing this?*"

"*Did she say this?*" asked Lenin. Amal turned towards him and said," *She behaves!*" Before Lenin could respond a gentle voice arose in the class.

Dr.Deepa Ramanathan, a woman with a kind heart; who treats every student with equal respect, never gets tired of teaching, and is the one who spices up her classes with a pinch of sarcasm.

"*Now, Lenin and Amal will perform this topic for you all*", she said.

"*Did she notice?*", Amal asked with a shocked face. "*She behaves*", he said.

Lenin and Amal walked to the vantage point facing their classmates. Amal had no awareness of the day's discussion except for the title "*Empathy*". Lenin, who remains a dumbass in class, had no clue.

"*Yes... You can start*", she said.

Amal with an awkward face asked, "*From where do we need to start, Mam?*"

"*Your wish, guys!*", she smiled.

Lenin turned towards the white screen that displayed the PPT gleaming from the projector and read the content. He saw the headings self-awareness, anger management and some notes on empathy. Using the hints from the topics he prepared an executive summary without any prior knowledge. He turned and asked, "*Kindly provide us some scenario Mam!*"

"*So, you figured it out, Lenin*", she asked.

"*I hope so*", he said with a freaky smile.

"*Okay, let's take it this way; Amal will act as an arrogant manager and Lenin, the employee who is seeking for a day off. Go ahead guys, Do it like a play*".

Lenin sat face-to-face with Amal, his position being diagonal to Haya. Amal began with a quizzical expression, along with a raised brow. "*Yes Lenin! What is the purpose of your visit?*"

Including Amal all the eyes were on Lenin, but he had his eyes on Haya. "*Your dress color suits you!*"

Haya stared back and Amal blushed, "*Is it so? Thanks bro*"

"*Ahem... Ahem... I think it is supposed to be a serious play*", said Dr.Deepa.

Amal went back to the character and asked, "*Excuse me! Answer my question?*"

Lenin began again "I *came here for a proposal of....*" Suddenly he zoomed out his vision from Haya's place as it was Dr.Deepa standing in front of Haya who signaled him to focus on the play.

Lenin had no option and went back to the play. "*Is it a good time to have a discussion sir?*"

Dr.Deepa began, "*Wait ! Everyone notice here; this is one good way of examining empathy*"

"*Empathy is the ability to sense other people's emotions, coupled with the ability to imagine what someone else might be thinking or feeling. If you are not clear with the emotion of the concerned persons just shoot out this question; it will help you to explore*" Dr.Deepa went on with the details of the scenario with the proceeds of the play. At the play's closure she said, " *Thanks Amal and Lenin. You can get back to your places. I want everyone to focus keenly on this topic and mainly you Mr. Lenin*".

She turned towards the PPT and continued the explanation.

"*So basically empathy focuses on other person's emotions, senses and predicament. Let me share some tips to improve empathy while communicating with others;*

Watch keenly and do not crosstalk until they complete the explanation.

Be fully present when you are with people and watch out for non-verbal cues.

Smile genuinely at the person with whom you are communicating.

Use their full Name to address them.

Try to empathize with people whose beliefs you don't share.

Give them some genuine recognition to make them comfortable.

Mainly, express gratitude from your side until the conversation ends.

Feel free and challenge yourself to have a deeper conversation."

The whole class was engaged in the interactive session headed by Dr. Deepa. She explained the tips with live examples and the do's and don'ts for empathy. When the clock struck 3:00 PM, she said, "*Oh, it's time*! That's enough for today"

The whole class started to shout "*Mam, that's not enough. You can continue your session.*"

Dr. Deepa " *Oh my dear! Im heading out for a personal work and will be unavailable for the next 1 week. I have mailed you the notes about the emotional framework. Kindly go through it and come up with an example for the next session. Take care, my dear students.*"

Everyone were about to get dispersed. Lenin was planning a hangout with his friends "*So what's up for today? Ceventers or McD?*" he asked his friends. A voice came from behind him, "*Roadside shop for Bhelpuri*" He turned and stared at Vega.

"*Okay you may go there. We shall hangout somewhere else bro!*" Amal replied angrily. Another suggestion came up, "*How about my house, for the tea break?*" It was Aaron, a healthy-food lover. While these guys were focusing on various dishes, one among his friends Ishika, a petite, short-tempered, good looking freaky girl kept on taking notes regardless of the session's closure. *"Hello Madam, It's over, can you hear me?"* asked Amal. *"Oh come on guys, Suggest some good place, I am starving!"* shouted Lenin.

"Ah... Coffee!" the sound came from another gang discussing near the class entrance. It was Haya; Haya Marium, a tall and fair girl with specs and a high pony tail complementing her beauty. She is straight forward and practical in both her vision and personal life.

Amal turned and searched, *"Lenin!"* Lenin was standing right at main door and said,

"Yes Haya, We shall"

"Okay guys, I will catch you all after the coffee. See you!", he fled away leaving Amal furious.

After about an hour, Lenin was in the parking lot of his college, controlling his tears and craving for a dear one to extend their moral support. He felt restless and whispered *"Am I... the one? I could never tell whether anyone really gets me"*.

Suddenly he felt the vibration in his left pant pocket and reached out for his mobile. It was Michael coincidentally expressing a green signal for him. On seeing the name in the caller ID, Lenin cleared his throat and screamed out *"Dude!"*

Yellow & Blue

(Sunshine, creative & Happiness) And (Cool, Funny & Charming)

"Buddy!", a guy in blue shirt came smiling into the cafeteria of the IT Company located in south Chennai. Yash, a slim & fit organized person and also a Guitarist

was sitting alone in the centremost table, watching the IPL highlights of CSK matches in the LCD TV hanging straight ahead of him. He turned around to find Parikshith, a funny, charming obedient man with a well-maintained physique, nerd guy but not with his mind, medium height and freaky voice that make you laugh within a second.

" *Hi Bonny!*", gestured Parikshith and sat near Yash, one lean and professional looking gentleman who takes every seconds as crucial like detonating a time bomb.

"*Stop using that!*"

"*It was the term coined by the giant Hippi and Robot, the great* "

"*Did they call you?*"

" *No! Did you get a call?*"

It was in that exact moment, Parikshith received a conference call with Lenin and Micheal on line and Yash around, thereby connecting all four.

" *Creeps! What's up?*", asked Parikshith.

"*Did you guys see the group?*", asked Micheal.

"*Nope, I didn't switch on the Data dude!*", said Lenin.

"*Because you don't have it!*", replied Parikshith.

"*Samyuktha is planning a trip*" said Michael.

"*And what's the budget?*" asked Yash.

"*The idea just evolved and the details are not confirmed yet*", said Micheal.

Being ignorant to Micheal's reply Yash went on, "*Where, when and how many of us are coming?*"

Lenin smiled and said, "*Mr. Perfect, Kindly gives some time to submit the report*".

"*See, I don't like spending money on this! Only if it is below 12K I will able to make it!*", Yash made a firm point.

Lenin "*What 12K? I don't think we will be engaging in that kind of a grand tour. Probably it might come around 7k*"

"*Hold on guys! Today is May 26*th *Friday. Let's have a conference call on May 28*th*; Sunday night*", Micheal concluded.

"*A video conference would be cool*", said Parikshith.

"*Whatever! Ping me before the call!*", said Yash.

"*Dudes! Let kill this remaining piece of shit in this trip. Always behaving like an OCD patient*", muttered Lenin.

Yash cut the call. "*That's rude, Bonny!*", said Parikshith.

Without a reply Yash turned on the data. There was a plenty of unread text as he didn't pay attention to the digital world for a while now. Among all the texts, he opened only one chat; Renukha. A bunch of unread messages stood there. He wanted to reply but he didn't. An internal force named ego restrained him from typing. Suddenly a new text message popped on the screen, "*Sorry Yash. I am really sorry. I know I had hurt you. I am sorry. I don't want to leave you but I was left with no other option*".

He was a lot tempted to reply and to avoid it he switched off the data. When he turned around he saw the other committed freak Parikshith.He is always spotted with a blue tooth headset. He has a hacker outlook but is not so; he is rather a Romeo. He was pampering his girlfriend in the phone call.

With a pleasant voice Parikshith went on," *Honey, we are planning for a trip. What? I would love to have you beside me but you know; these boys won't leave me alone in trip. Let me figure the spot and if it is worthy, we shall assign it for our honey moon trip!*"

Yash tapped on Parikshith shoulder, "*She?*"

"*Yeah Bonny, You want to talk?*", asked Parikshith.

"*No, Have fun!*". He gave a warm hug and walked towards his cubicle

Purple

(Royalty, Wealthy & ambitious)

It was 7 P.M on a weekend time where modern youths begin to party. Meanwhile, in the heart of Gachibowli, stood an IT-banking firmoffice ; on the 10th floor of which a team of six members were rushing to attend the scrum call of the week. Everyone assembled at the conference room; the only room that was lit on the entire building.

Skype's calling tune rang and Mark Westbrook from US attended the call "*Hi all! Hello!*"

"*Hi Mark!*". The pretty much lovable woman with his fair and impressive face cut, where men had gone mad over with her visionary speech ; her dressing sense is a one solid reason to make everyone to love her, groomed in a formal white shirt and black pencil skirt with her let-open coloured locks dangling around, sat cross-legged with a pen spinning around her fingers. "*Good Morning! This is Hansi from compensation team. I am here with my teammates for the weekly report submission*"

"*Yes Hansi! You may continue!*"

"*Mark, we need to reconsider this week e-filing analytics. We are facing an issue from your BI analytics tools. I request you to kindly forward your credentials with which we can move on to validation phase*"

"*Issues! As in?*"

Hansi continued,"*Fetching data error due to the insertion query*".

"*Yeah right! We are working on it. What about the verification?*"

"*We are completed with that and the mail will be sent once we are cleared with the validation part*", said Ankit; a team member of Hansi.

"Yeah! Sounds great! We'll forward the credentials".

"Boss we have already gotten into the night hours of Friday", said another team member.

Ankit signals him to shut up and continued, " *That's it for this week from our side. Any other queries from your end?"*

"It looks like we are also done for the week! Happy weekend guys!"

"Yeah! Thank you Mark, Happy weekend!", said Ankit.

After the beep of ending the call sounds all the six heaved a great sign of relief.

Hansi returned to her desk and was collecting her belongings to leave for the day. "Hansi! Beer?" She turned towards Siva, a teammate and a good friend of her. He even tried to promote her friendship but it appeared like Hansi escaped from the love laboratory not wanting to be anywhere around it. "Yes! I need one. Shall we?"

Hansi and Shiva reached the Resto bar in Shiva's Volkswagen car. Siva opened the door for Hansi and walked towards the table. "Hope you like this place!", initiated Siva.

Suddenly a waitress appeared before them. *"Hi Mam! Why are you so late? As usual you're favourite Heineken, right? "*

"Yes, One for me and you Shiva?"

The stunned Siva blabbered, *"Ah, ah, I want, I need..."*

"Hey you want hot or soft drinks?", she asked

"I'll go with brandy, one Antiquity please!"

" That's whiskey, Shiva!"

" Oh! So they started product diversification. That's good! Then, make it as two Heineken!". Hansi and waitress laughed.

"Hansi, you look fabulous in this purple top", he tried to restart.

"Oh! Without this purple outfit, I might appear average right?"

Shiva ignored that comment and tried to get straight to the point, *"Ah! Hansi, I am..."*

"You love me" Hansi placed a full stop to his sentence.

"Yes!", he said with his head bowed down.

The waitress returned with their order, *"Here, your order mam! And compliment beverage"*

Hansi took the first sip and asked, *"What kind of reply do you expect from me, Shiva?"*

"Anything, but be honest!"

Hansi took another sip and said,*"Hmmm. Honestly, I don't love you!"*

"Why?"

"You expect an honest answer and you can't accept the honesty from a women".

"I am leaving". The agitated Siva opened his wallet and paid for the drinks .

"Hey! Doesn't matter! I'll pay. You are my friend".

"Not mandatorily required", Siva said in an angry tone and turned around to leave.

"Shiva! I am committed!", she said. He took few seconds to pause but without turning back and a further word he walked away, his pace getting faster as if running out of Hansi's sight.

Hansi drank the beer completely and enjoyed the snacks solely. She bid adieu with the waitress came out from the lounge. She saw some youngsters smoking in a corner. She approached them and asked, *"Lighter?"* and one among them gave it to her.

Amidst the smoke from her cigarette she took out her mobile and switched it on. She saw 10 missed calls from Samyuktha and some unread message in Gryffindors group.

She saw the text "*Trip?*" from Samyuktha. "*Impossible!*" Hansi muttered, dropped her cigarette and typed without even reading the following messages.

"*I am IN*"- 9:15 PM

Violet

(Magic, Mystery & Extravagance)

"*Ayesha, have you gone to sleep?*", screamed her mother.

A well-read urban city girl, with neatly plaited hair was hearing songs in her violet Bluetooth headset with high volume unaware of her mother's chiding. Her furious mother came to her room and gave her a tight slap.

"*Mom! I did nothing to get slapped?*" Ayesha screamed. Ayesha a nerd but a trustworthy resource and innocent girl who wear specs; she is medium height and a good looking shape with a corn row hairstyle, with violet frame specs who remains half-minded and always sing songs is the main reason for the hues to stay united.

The screams of the mother-daughter duo echoed in their colony in Tuticorin. "You do nothing and that's the problem now" her mom replied and came the train of advices. "If this is the way of your being active in prime time, how are you going to survive in your in-laws home? Do you know our culture? How a woman should be on her toes in evening time when everyone is at home. And look at you! If this habit continues no man will come forward to marry you. Act as a matured one".

"*Why are you cursing me?*", she asked as tears rolled down uncontrollably.

Ayesha is a typical south Indian girl, born and brought up in a conventional orthodox family where a girl taking a own stand and make her own decisions were unheard of.

She was grown with an intense family bonding pampered with lots of care and affection.

After the dispute being put to bed, the family gathered for the last meal of the day, seated around the dine-in table. She had an younger brother named Insaf, doing second year undergrad.

Her brother with an intention to irritate her asked, *"Dad! Any alliances?* "

Ayesha's father after taking a Dosa said, " *Any? There are many; it's my princess who needs to choose her prince*". Ayesha's face went to low battery mode." Choice is yours papa!"

"See, that's my daughter! She never lets me down"

"Do I have any option?", she muttered for which her brother and mother laughed .

Ayesha signalled her brother to share his hotspot.

"I'll but for that you need to draw two diagrams in my record note. Will you?", he whishpered. "*Damn! I will*", she said.

With one hand on food and other hand under the table the siblings share their mobile data and using their mobiles like chits in exam.

When Ayesha switched on the Data, she received the messages only from Gryffindor. She saw the last text from Hansi.

"I am IN"- 9:15 PM

Without glancing at the earlier messages she replied back.

"Me too"- 09:30 PM

CHAPTER II

Temperature

Trip Day 1: June 12th Morning-6:45 AM, Electronic city, Bangalore.

The seventh floor of a luxurious apartment in the Electronic city is the inception point for the Hues trip which is supposedly the residence of modern age Josh Gosling, Michael. The hues gathered in the techno freak flat which was furnished with play stations, computer quotes, dispersed eatable packets on the floor, condoms, 24/7 turned on AC and scattered paper works. Everyone was having a quick refresh; while the smokers Lenin and Micheal isolated themselves and took a walk to have a puff. Michael took a long walk to a private placewhere Lenin fainted out "*Dude! I thought this would be an memorable trip but you haven't mentioned that it begins with a Yatra*"

(*Yatra- A Journey held by Saints)

After settling on a spot in the parking lane of a mall, Micheal took out the branded Dunhill and passed to Lenin.

"*Dude, Did Samyuktha broke up with Laxman?*", questioned Lenin after the strange journey last night.

"*May be or may be not*", he replied in a who-cares tone.

"*You never change Mr. Playboy. Alright! Now tell me what made you to help me?*"

"*What did I do?*"

Color Splash: Green

On the $5^{th}$of June, a Monday, where the whole city appears to run in an ultra fast-forward motion, Michael was laying half-conscious and hung over in his favorite bean bag unable to open up his eyes.

The doorbell rang like an alarm and he slowly got up from the bed, crawling over to the main door. He viewed the camera footage on the TV screen in the living room.

"Oh Shit!", he muttered and looked at the clock. It was 11:00 A.M."She'sgonna bury me with her words", he thought and rushed to his living room. He wore his yet to be ironed formal shirt and trousers and ran to open the door, making a decent hair-do on the way with bare hands. On opening the door,"Babe! I got held up with work for a while. But look, I am getting ready for meetingyour parents", apologized Micheal with a gentle English accent.

"Today is our compensation off, Michael",Aishu raised her base voice. Aishu, Michael's teammate and girlfriend were in the progress for getting married but Michael was one typical IT cool freak who doesn't want to feel congested in the orthodox spidery web.

"Work from Home!" Michael replied.

"Fuck Off!" She turned around and took a few steps in the corridor expecting him to seek her. But Micheal closed the door and went inside. She banged the door open and found him lying on his bean bag.

"You haven't changed a bit. My parents were waiting for you for more than an hour. If it were your parents would you behave in the same way?"

"Nope!My parents won't expect punctuality from me"

"Listen now! I can't tolerate this anymore. Let's..." Aishuwas stuck with a pause in her words.

"Breakfast?" Michael casually replied.

She crossed her hands with anger and tears flaring in her eyes.

"Babe, Why are you doing this to me?", he asked and moved close to her leaving only half inch gap and was slowly reaching her lips. "Babe no!", she said and her breathing was getting

heavier. His hands went behind her. "Lighter?", he asked showing the one that he fetched from the cupboard behind.

"Go to hell!", she thundered and left the flat.

After the civil war, Michael went to the restroom, placed his mobile in the mobile stand that was fixed next to the wash basin. Simultaneously, he was brushing his teeth and checking his phone. He found 275 texts in Gryffindor group. He opened from the middle.

***Samyuktha**" Hey! Listen we are all grown up. We have to understand the situationhere " 9:32 AM*

***Lenin**" Without organizer how can we go ahead?" 9:33AM*

***Ayesha**" That's why, she booked a resort for six from her own coupons" 9:34 AM*

***Parikshith**"So, accommodation comes free of cost! Sound's good" 9:35 AM*

***Lenin**" Shut up man! That's unfair! Friends should be a part of every memorable moment" 9:40 AM*

***Lenin** "Just recall! How our college days were like......" 9:40 AM*

Samyuktha left

Ayesha left

Parikshith left

***Yash** "Lenin, I beg you! Please stop your lecture. I am gonna add them back" 9:43 AM*

Yash added Samyuktha

Yash added Ayesha

Yash added Parikshith

***Yash**"Guys! Let me calculate the expenses per head and we shall split the work" 9:45 AM*

Michael scrolled the chat and found something fishy. He moves to the last 10 texts in the group.

***Yash** "Sam, we need to spend a minimum of 7K per head. To make things comfortable and face contingency, 10K per head would do" 10:49 AM*

***Samyuktha**" Sound's logical. Guys what's up?" 10:51 AM*

***Parikshith**"Yes, I am fine with this budget" 10:53 AM*

***Ayesha** "Yeah me too!" 10: 55 AM*

***Samyuktha**"Lenin?" 10:57 AM*

***Yash**"Lenin, Waiting for your order man" 10: 58 AM*

***Samyuktha** "It's you and Michael whose approval is pending" 10:59 AM*

***Ayesha** "Sam, leave Mike; he will accept whatever be the budget" 10:53 AM*

***Yash** "I think he is still in hangover mode" 10:55 AM*

***Lenin** "10K? That's too..., "10:57 AM*

***Samyuktha**" Too?" 10:58 AM*

***Lenin** " Yeah! That's okay!" 10:59 AM*

Michael immediately called Lenin. He was preparing for internal viva with his friends in the exam hall. " Hey Robot!"

" Hey Hippi!",Micheal called out amidst brushing his teeth.

"Dude, your voice is breaking!" Lenin answered

He spat and rinsed his mouth. "How much do you have?"

"Have what?"

"I asked how much have you allotted for the trip?"

"Hey! I have enough money dude. That's not a problem!"

"Then, quote the amount".

"Dude, I have" Lenin was limping in his words.

"Lenin, I know you. You won't spend much neither bother your parents. At last you will turn down the trip. It's not gonna work here. Not with me. Now, quote the amount that you can set aside for the trip".

After a pause Lenin said,"7K".

Both remained muted on the call and in 30 seconds Lenin received a message.

Michael R has credited Rs 5,000 in your ICICB Bank account ********0765 Now, available balance is Rs 12,000. You can access the account details in below link*** www.wtyrnc.icicb

"Dude! There is an additional 2K",asked Lenin.

"It's for our booze and smoke buddy! Return it with a bang" Michael laughed and cut the call.

Michael *"Consider it done!" 11:45 AM*

Lenin *"#MetooJ" 11:46 AM*

"*What did I do?*",Micheal asked. "*That's because it was you, "Hippi!"*, he thought.

Lenin punched on his arms and said "*Fucking fellowhip!*"

Lenin received a call; Michael crushed his half-finished cigarette and grabbed his mobile. "*Time's up! We need to move on*"

"*Hey wait! That's my mobile*".

"*Yeah I know. See our mooz car reached the destination*"

"*What? You gave my number?*",Lenin asked with a raised eyebrow.

"*And you are going to submit the original license Hippi!*". He answered the call and waved his hand; on the sign of which arrived two cars – brand new and well-maintained in the parking lot before them.

"*Swift or Figo?*" Michael asked.

After about an hour everyone was done and about to take off except for Micheal and Lenin who were leisurely getting ready amidst the chit-chat.

"*What are all the tools you are focus for process mining?*", Michael questioned.

"*Kitchen knife*",Samyuktha replied by holding one over his throat. "*What are you both thinking? Getting ready for a date? It doesn't even matter if you drive naked!"*

"Oh! Is it so?", Lenin's face brightened in the middle of his outfit search.

"Cut the crap man", said Yash. *"Mind your words with these dirty minds, Sam"*.

After a few minutes Lenin appeared in a cargo shorts and loose-fitted t-shirt. *"Are we good?"*

"Your age is reduced to half", said Parikshith stunned by his look.

After the fun chats, and pleasant prayers the perfectly packed Hues geared up towards the south direction from Bangalore via Mysore and was reaching the state border. Michael was driving swift with Ayesha, Samyuktha and Parikshith.Figo was packed with Yash along with the 24/7 starving souls- Hansi and Lenin, who made frequent stoppings to satiate their hunger. But Michael is one good destination-oriented driver whostops the vehicle only on the reaching spot just like an Uber driver.

They travelled through Channapatna highway, the route which is being also used frequently by elephants and deer. Having escaped from the routine of staring at their system screen for hours and over-whelming pressure into the wild with trees lined up on both sides playing hide and seek with the sun rays that tends to streak into the forest in the presence of desired people gave pure delight to the hues.

The hues were enjoying the trip and taking snaps in-between with the wildlife photographer Lenin. There was a police check post in Kerala border and none of the hues except Lenin had the teeny bit of idea about the liquor bottles in Figo that was a few minutes away.

Michael slowed down the car,

As if seated in an exam hall Parikshith whispered, "Dude! You never mentioned about the checking in borders."

"*Chill!Chill !*", smiled Micheal.

"*Oh! We shall get through this*", said Sam.

The police officer asked them to get down. Sam was trying to wake the dozy Ayesha, "*Hey! Uncle is calling you*".

"*Uncle!*", said Ayesha.

"*Hello Mam!Please get down*".

Ayesha freaked out and repeated "*Uncle!*"

"*Oh! Shut up Granny!*", muttered Sam.

Micheal handed over the papers to a middle-aged cop who began the interrogation. Ayesha was terrified whileSamyuktha and Parikshith were stunned as to how an old monk drunken could be so calm in the police checking scene.

"*Where are you coming from?*", asked the cop.

"*Bangalore*" he replied.

"*And going to?*"

"*Wayanad*" he replied with a smile.

"People usually plan trips on the weekends but you different bunch have planned on the weekdays", he said and went on to write the vehicle number in the register.

Where they were waiting near the booth for the formalities to get done, Parikshith asked, "*Mike! Promise me that you don't have any liquor?*"

"*I Promise you. I have two large Scotch and six beers, added with one pack of Dunhill*", said Micheal.

"*What the hell Mike!*",Samyuktha asked with an angry bird face.

"*Chill guys! They are safe and not to worry about*", he replied.

"*Please don't play with us!*",Ayesha started to cry.

"*Guys! I have kept in Lenin car's, below the baggage. They are heading towards Mysore road where will either be less checking or none, since it is working day"*, Micheal winked.

"*That's my Man!*" Parikshith hugged him tightly.

"*Guys!The Cop is coming*", Ayesha wiped her tears.

"*Here are your papers. Travel safely*", said the Cop.

When his hands reached for the papers, Michael saw a car approaching and froze in shock; so did the entire bunch. A guy from brand new Figo was asking the cop, "Sir! Is this the route to Wayanad?" It was Lenin in the car driven by Hansi with Yash sleeping in the backseat with his headset on.

Michael and team stood there like statues. The cop turned towards Figo and began his interrogation part two, "Get down the car please!" Suddenly Yash from the backseat asked, "*Hey you guys are waiting for us here?*" Four of them nodded their head in slow motion indicating a Yes.

"*So you know them?*", asked the cop.

"*Yes sir!*", replied Michael |"*No sir!*", replied Ayesha

"*Yes or No?*", the Cop smiled and asks.

" *Yes sir!*", said Hansi. "W*e are friends and we are heading towards Wayanad for a trip. Any problem with that sir!*"

"*No Problem Mam. For security purpose we have collected your friends' vehicle number. Will you guys stick together for this trip?*"

"*Yes sir!*", replied Ayesha | "*No sir!*", replied Michael.

The cop laughed and said, "*Oh god! You people remind me of my college days. I am sure you are going to enjoy this one hell of trip.One car detail is enough. You may go now!*"

"*Go!*" said Michael's with a terrified face.

"*Let's go! Let's go!*", cried Sam. Parikshith and Ayesha smiled at the cop and said, "*Thanks a lot sir!*"

"*It is my duty! Take care and have a wonderful trip!*", the Cop replied and took out a cigarette from his pocket, searching for lighter.

“*Here sir!*”, came a hand holding the lighter.

“*Oh! Thank you*”, he lit the cigar and was surprised on seeing the owner.

“*No mention officer*”, Hansi smiled and walked back towards the Figo.

The Hues entered the God’s own country with a pleasant change in the weather welcoming rain drops to crash on the ground; the ambience elevating their ecstasy.

CHAPTER III

Spectral V/s Non-Spectral

12th June Monday 3:25 PM

The two cars crossed Bandipur forest area and entered Wayanad. They parked their vehicles near a tea shop which had a breath-taking hill view.

Hansi was leaning her left hand on rear mirror of Figo, Ayesha placed comfortable over Swift hood, Samyuktha opens the front door of Swift and to get placed in the front seat, Yash and Parikshith leaning over the two car's closed back door facing opposite to each other, Michael was standing facing the cars. Lenin was left somewhere enjoying his photography with seismic beauty.

"*We thought you would be held up in your project. How did you manage?*", Sam asked Hansi.

"*That's a long story; Mein Kampf. Leave it for now and tell me this. How did you guys sought permission?*"

Recalling their trick everyone went for quick flashback.

Rewind

June 5th Monday

The trip was planned on June 12thMonday to June 15th Thursday carrying weekend from past week it longs for seven days trip. Hansi was one independent woman considered for the plan after helping her giggles with a resort stay, it was left with the rest six members.

Coimbatore

"What? You are going with girls for the trip!", Lenin's big brother studying overseas laughed in the video call.

"Why?" Do you have any objection?", Lenin asked.

"I don't have! But our parents might have", Rishi said. "Now tell me, what is your strategy? How are you planning to sought their permission ?"

Tuticorin

"Vapa, Please!I need to spend time with my friends!", Ayesha pleaded to her father.

"Why don't you spend your holiday with us!" Her dad intentions rise slowly.

"Vapa, I am already spending day and night with you people. Isn't it fair for my side to ask for some time with my friends?", she replied.

"Hey! Mind your Language?", Her mom pounded on her.

Chennai

"Pervert!", accused Parikshith' girlfriend.

"Honey! They are my friends. You know them right?",Parikshith with his sweet voice tried to convince her along with kisses in-between the convo.

"Okay! How many days will you be unavailable?"

"Just four days!", he answered in low volume.

Bangalore

"Four days? That's impossible Mike!" , said Gowtham, Michael's colleague reacts.

"Why not?"

"One, You are the critical resource and two, you are single. Our Manager won't allow you for this, at any cost".

"Okay! Now instead of being pessimistic, suggest me a way out".

Coimbatore

"Listen! Don't tell to our parents that you are going with girls. Tell them that you are going for a photography contest. And don't ever mention the actual location", advised Lenin's big brother.

"Why shouldn't I mention the spot?"

"To get approval, don't ever use a hill station. A gentle remainder!"

"Roger that! Commander", Lenin laughed.

Chennai

"So, you are all set for trip?", asked Vidya.

"I hope so! I wish none of the other idiots makes it a flop show", Said Sam.

"It's gonna be a big hit."

"They are the ones who cause more trouble as well as the peak of joy. My rainbow in the sky", she smiled.

"Who's accompanying you?"

South Chennai

"No! Please leave me alone", Yash thundered with.

Renukha was standing beside him expecting to be forgiven. "I feel very guilty now."

"You better be! Now tell me, did I propose to have a date with you?"

"No"

"Then?" He took a minute silence and continued. "You girls, spend time with a guy, have fun, give him an imaginary fairy tale making him believe it's so real and ever-lasting and all of a sudden throw it off as if it doesn't matter anymore."

"Yash! Can you not shout?",Renukha's eyes went teary.

"Why the hell should I? Do you really have an idea of what you meant to me?"

"I know Yash. But it's my parents. They mean the world to me".

"What about me then?", his voice went breaking.

"I loved you a lot."

"Just go away Renu. Don't ever try to meet me" he turned to walk away.

She held his hands and cried, "Please! Forgive me Yash. You are important to me but I can't stay with you forever".

He let go of her hand and walked away.

Coimbatore

"Whatever happens please don't weep in front of mom that's important!" Rishi spells out his final advice."Why?" Lenin can't get any option. Rishi continue to explain" Because our mom hates when we shed tears and surely figure out that we are curious to do that thing then approximately.." "Yeah... yeah... I got it, Thanks a lot Biggie!" Lenin with a smile

Tuticorin

"Don't show-off with that smiley face of yours", said Ayesha's younger brother.

"I will! Can't you see? I am going on a trip with my Toots", Ayesha laughed.

"Wait! Your toots?It means including boys? Vapa?"

She shut his mouth and whispered. "If you ever disclose this then I will whistle blow your smoking stuff"

"Got it! A valid point! But still I can't believe that you got permission from him".

"Even I couldn't"

Bangalore

"Even I couldn't handle the stress regarding our last project, Mike", said Michael's manager.

"That's why I am looking forward to the devotional trip boss"

"Maybe you are right, Mike. Take your off and refresh yourself."

"Boss, is it for real?", he asked surprisingly.

"Not unless you want me to cancel it?"

Michael thanked him and came out to his regular smoking area. He took out his mobile to update his approval.

Michael *"Guys Finally I got the approval!" 3:00 PM*

Samyuktha *"Awesome Robot!" 3:02 PM*

Parikshith *"I am always with you guys ;)"3:03 PM*

Lenin *"Hey Baby! We know you man! You cupid stupid!"3:04 PM*

Ayesha *"Guys! I am very happy that I got permission from my Dad" 3:05 PM*

Lenin *"That's impossible!" 3:06 PM*

Samyuktha*" Ahem! Mr. Bonny are you there?" 3:07 PM*

Parikshith *"Hey!I guess he is in a meeting. He will surely come and I'll take care of it" 3:08 PM*

Lenin *"Guys! We are finally in mutual wavelength and that's great to hear" 3:09 PM*

Samyuktha *"Hasta la Vista" 3:10 PM*

CHAPTER IV

Harmony

Samyuktha breathes in the fresh air and with a sip of that Kerala special black tea she breathes out "At last, I am with you guys. I need to spend a lot and share many memories with you!" Michael interfered "Much more than memories, crazy stuff will burst out for upcoming three days." Hansi points her finger at Lenin "Like this!" He was capturing a monkey imitating just like how he holds his own camera, "Hence proved, we are Primates" Samyuktha replied sarcastically.

Around 4 to 5 PM, two cars drove past a dark forest area into a sun faded evening, with a soft light tone. They were in search of the Resort they booked. An isolated wood house welcomes our hues with an old man standing in front of the opening gate. They have a parking lot to hold approximately two cars. In a closed compound, surrounded by large palm trees, Resort had one main building and a swimming pool behind it. A dense pathway with a line of bricks in which only a single person can walk on, leads to that swimming pool. There were foot stairs close to the pool that gave way to a tree house which serves as the dining block for the resort with a fine dining and also BBQ setup for eight members. Mainly at the edge of the block, there was a large balcony which stunned Lenin "Awwww, what a pleasing scenery view!" he said, viewing the complete Wayanad forest with his 50mm camera Lens.

The main building consists of one living room including a large sofa with two sofa chair, an LCD TV, two bedrooms to the left and the right corners. A small dining hall was attached to the living room, to the left a wash basin for brushing and towards right there was a path over the path, way more right side was the washroom with one cupboard and a single cot to its left. There was a loft above with a small dining hall where four beds were placed looking clumsy and comfortable for closed friends to make their beautiful chit chats.

Fore evening 7 PM, Hues sat at the dining table and discussed their trip agenda that was planned by the stressful organizer Yash, "See guys, we need to be on time!" he says, placing the travel guide on the table. "On your lead, Master" Lenin bows goodnaturedly.

"Day 1: Chembra peak & Ripon tea factory

Day 2: Edakkal cave, Jain temple"

Immediately Lenin's face switches off, everyone looks back and forth between him and Yash.

"*Hey! That's not in our plan. The second day, we are going to Pakshipathalam Bird sanctuary and Karlad Lake*" Yash replies and smiles after seeing him.

"*Hail Bonny!*" everyone shouts to cheer his unimaginable plan with our colors.

They split their dinner from the kitchen served by beloved oldies who are in charge of the resort. At the same time, Yash and Michael placed chairs nearby to Lenin who was scrolling through the photos in his camera. "*Could you kindly lend us your time, Mr. Wildlife photographer,*" Michael says, urging him to chat. "*You know what, we miss our Lenin. Lenin who disturbs us 24/7 with his stupid advices, the one who takes care of us, the one who blabbers with us and with us only. Is he alive?*" Yash piped in by slinging his right arm over his shoulder.

Lenin smiles back at them, his eyes brimming with tears. Michael understands that he is trying to control himself

"Dude! Smoke?" Lenin knocks their heads against each other with a "Nope." Samyuktha who was sitting beside them, watching the scene silently, signals for them to settle down while she calls everyone and opens up the beer "*Guys let's just chill with the climate*"

Everyone picked up their beer. There were some crispy chicken BBQ with Roti, Paneer butter, and Ghee rice served on the table. They were ready to cheer when Michael started his honorary speech "Guys, thanks to everyone who made this happen. We are finally here. It's been almost 9 years, we are all together for a whole load of fun, problems, celebrations, and of course some career brainstorming too. We'll still be connected in our upcoming years. To our friendship and madness, cheers!" Everyone roars with joy shouting "*Cheers!*"

Our hues glow even brighter after hearing tech savvy's blissful vote of thanks.

Samyuktha slowly turns to Ayesha with her words "Does anyone miss their home?" "Home!" immediately shouts Lenin with a stricken face."What's the time now?" he exclaims pulling Yash's right arm to peer at his watch for the time; it was 9:00 PM. "Fuck!" Lenin rushes to the living room where everyone's mobiles were charging. He opens the main door and finds his own mobile from the mess. And his face turns pale when notifications pops out.

"10 missed calls"

"15 missed Whatsapp voice calls"

Lenin seems to tense up and sweat as if he is standing in front of a highly complicated bomb. Samyuktha enters right behind him "What? Why did you rush over here, man. You sounded so serious." Lenin turns the phone to her, showing that he received calls from his beloved family and most of all from his dad. "Should I speak?" Ayesha suggests a requisition. "No Way!" Samyuktha shouts outloud. "Why?" Ayesha questioned.

Color Splash: Red

The night when Samyuktha and Lenin depart from Coimbatore. She was waiting at the arrival point with her luggages when Samyuktha received a one line text with a smiley of "Bon Voyage ☺ " from Krishna, an anonymous yet to be revealed. She smiles a little and opens the contact to call Red. Mobile rings and "Michael, You reached?" Lenin answers with an unexpected question in his voice.

"What? You Dumb! It's me, Sam" she replied.

"Oh that's good man! I will reach there in 5-10 mins!" Lenin shouts out loud. "5-10mins? Dude, the Bus is going to start now," she laughed waiting for him to get tense.

"Oh, is it so!? Bus is delayed, Dad, so we'll reach early" he winced and looked about ready to die.

"Lenin, you are still Dad's little prince. How charming!" she smiled and paused with growing curiosity.

Later when Lenin arrived with his Dad, Samyuktha understood the trick that friends of opposite genders should follow in front of a shy family. She moves from there and sits facing the wall. Lenin's Dad unintentionally places his seat facing the road right behind where Sam was seated.

"Hope you will sleep at a proper time and wake up early" says Lenin's Dad. Lenin replies "Yes Dad!"

"Don't forget to call us at 8PM every day" "Yes Dad!"

"Don't consume unhealthy foods, Okay?" "Yes Dad!"

"Watch out for the people you meet" "Yes Dad!"

"Do you love Haya?" Samyuktha interrupted their conversation "Yes Dad!" Lenin said without missing a beat.

Here though, The Minor Drawback for Sam and a major escape route for Lenin is that his Dad has not met any of his friends. Only his mother is aware about his complete friendship history. His Dad, as if hearing a spell from Sam simply says "And keep your distance from women, Okay?" Lenin still replies like a kindergarten kid "Yesssss Dad!"

At Present

Rishi, Lenin's elder brother begins with a scream "You! What did you say to Mom and Dad? Where have you gone? Can't you call our Dad before the party?" Lenin slowly opens up "Biggie, I was actually at a BBQ party, that's why I couldn't see my mobile. What did our dad say?"

"Stop right there! Let me make a conference call with our parents, and don't reply to anything dad says. Got it right?" He begins by helping out his brother. "Hello Dad, he is on the call too!"

Mr. Anand begins his archana* "*You fool! Rascal! How dare you keep your mobile away from you?*"

(*Archana refers to Mantra chanters to God)

"*Dad!*" Lenin tries. "*Shut up, man!*" Rishi warns again.

"*What?*" Mr. Anand asks.

Rishi exclaims "*I was just shouting at Lenin, Dad!*"

"*Well then, better to shout at him with some bad words. He deserves more than that.*" Rishi starts to defend his brother "*Dad! Calm down please. It wasn't his mistake. There's no network in Wayanad!*"

Mr. Anand, "*What? Wayanad! When did you go there? You said the trip is to Bangalore!*"

Lenin, "*Actually, Dad! He is kidding. Michael's area is down on signal. So he compared it with Wayanad where the signal is down too!*"

Mr. Anand, "*This doesn't seem fair. What are you both thinking?*"

Rishi, "*Wait Dad! You can't blame a person for fault in an electronic device!*"

Mr. Anand, "*But Rishi, I can blame the person who owns it, right?*"

Lenin "*I am sorry, Dad!*"

Normally parents hate themselves when they hear apologies from their children. They don't want to see their kids' heads down and feel sorry even if they did something wrong. In the same way Mr. Anand felt now. So he tried to calm himself.

Mr. Anand, "*Okay! We are tense; once your mobile is kept on waiting. I asked you to call me, right? Please don't repeat this, my child. Oh wait, your Mom wants to say something.*"

Mrs. Anand takes over the phone and it pleases him to hear her "*My dear! In case you are busy with your friends, call us early in the evening so that we won't disturb you. Sorry, if we disturbed you*"

Lenin, "*Mom! Don't say sorry to us!*"

Mrs. Anand, "*We feel the same way towards you! Now tell me the truth, where are you?*"

Rishi interrupts slowly "*Mom! He went to...*"

Lenin "*Wayanad*"

Rishi, "*Clean Bowled!*"

Mrs. Anand, "*Lenin, Who is accompanying you?*"

Rishi, "*Ahem... Ahem*"

Lenin, "*My friends, Mom.*"

Mrs. Anand, "*Girls as well?*"

Lenin, "*Yes, three of them!*"

Mrs. Anand, "*Why do you say the truth now?*"

Lenin replied, "*Because I believe you!*"

Mrs. Anand, "*Oh my dear, the trust that three girls have on you is more valuable than the trust you have on me.*"

Lenin replies with heads down "*hmm*"

Mrs. Anand, "*My little Communist, I didn't say that I feel for you!*"

Lenin, "*I am so proud that I raised a child who holds the trust of his fellow creatures*"

Rishi "*Is it so?*"

Mrs. Anand "*Now Rishi, why didn't you express this before?*"

Rishi tries to escape the counter strike "*Mom, I can't hear you! The signal breaks, what did you say?*"

All three of them start to laugh. Lenin can't even imagine that his mother opened up about him. Lenin understood that millennials basically get attracted towards their opposite gender with ease. But for every generation the trust blossoms through a friendship and it may be stronger than any relationship in their lifetime. That's the reason there are no synonyms for the word break up between friends.

The beloved conversations between the mom and sons end. Lenin and the hues take their beds from the room and leave the ones at the loft. With all the tiredness of making this long journey, Michael and Lenin fall asleep while the rest of the colors all lay down and start humming their favorite song from the Money Heist series.

"Una mattina mi sono alzato
O bella ciao, bella ciao, bella ciao, ciao, ciao"

CHAPTER V

Shade

Trip Day2: June 13th Tuesday 7:45 AM, A pleasant Sunrise rays fall over the loft that made colors to witness and enjoy the day begin with a friendship blast after a long day. They have been doing this in their college days particularly their IV periods.

Samyuktha, Ayesha woke up and made Yash a shake and signals watch Michael and Lenin, meanwhile, Hansi was in mild sleep receives the signal, they were waiting for one prey from two. When Michael woke up they fell over Lenin's shouts to tear his eardrum "*Good Morning Buddy!*"

It was a post-breakfast session; they were packing for one-day trek to Chembrapak, Wayanad's famous peak, said to be the tallest in Wayanad, with a height of 2,100 meters above sea level that offers a great spot for exercising adventure and thrills for nature lovers. There are many exotic spices in this part of traveling to a breathtaking view mixed with flora and fauna.

Two cars went to a limit and travelers need to walk for almost 1.5 to 2 kilometers then trek starts for the Chembra peak. Their adventures begin from the very first parking lot, where everyone walks fast to the hill, Michael and Lenin pulls Ayesha to wait for them after the remaining colors sparks out

"I doubt that Laxman and Samyuktha broke up each other" Lenin questions. Ayesha replied "*Even me too, why can't you ask her*" "*We had a fear of what if she gets hurts*" Michael expresses the typical boys feeling tied up in an opposite gender friendship.

"*Guys, We won't get hurt if you are open, But we will when you hide your thoughts about us*" Ayesha place her arm over their shoulders "*Now, Whatever you felt you can open up! You assholes*" Ayesha laughs and hits on Michael's backbone.

"*Ah! Lenin, Watch out! Lenin*" said Michael and turns aside. Lenin was faded out and he searches, Ayesha, turns his face over the hill area where our hues walking forward meanwhile Lenin was rushing towards Sam to witness the mystery till now about the relationship of their behold buddy.

Chembra peak beginning part seems to be too close but if you miss your people within the nearer distance you can meet them only at the top hill viewpoint. When Ayesha and Michael came close to the take-off stage of the hill, they saw a big giant with the camera, Lenin sat on a large stone with whole sweating over the loose t-shirt.

"Hey... Got your relationship advice?" Ayesha laughs for a while gave a HiFi. "*Nope, I was waiting for you guys*" he replied "*Dude! Is that peak too far from here*" Michael looks over the hilltop with a freak-out face "*I dunno, better you people stick with me too close*" Lenin takes a long breathe to reply. Ayesha alerts them "*Yep, even signals won't work properly, I think so*"

The Remaining reached the hilltop and was looking for these three colors, at last when they reached the half of track "*Dude! Look over here*" Michael moves aside and stands over top of a rock. It pictures with Wayanad surround by breezy clouds with wholesome of greenery view, fresh air from monsoon feels to breathe like living in Heaven. "*Smash the view*" Lenin takes over his camera to snap the nature shot. Michael starts to pour out his internal talks "*Dude! I feel so jealous that these people are born with blessings... What an environment man*". Ayesha freezes for a second and had only a few words to utter "*God's Own Country*"

Yash shouts out loud "*Heyy, who made this choice!*" Samyuktha replied, "*Hansi, Why?*" They witness the craziness from him he moves over to her and hugs her meanwhile Parikshith and Samyuktha hold them too. They were standing in front of the Hearten shape lake that is located on the edge and placed as an interface region of two hills. They saw their reflection in the lake and their face automatically pitches a smile for this present. "*This is the best day in my life*" Samyuktha utters inside.

"*Sam, this would be the best place for your Honeymoon*" Lenin, who stands behind them. Ayesha came and speak out with breathing "*This was a most wanted statement that he wishes to deliver starting from the day*". Samyuktha stays silent and watches over Lenin for almost 10 seconds then she takes a deep breath. She tries to control but the fresh air is blown over the top view, birds sound, and naturist situation made her pour tears along with her internal wound "*Laxman is dead!*"

All of sudden, Complete Colors went to statue mode they haven't expect this kind of response from her. Ayesha accompanies them during their college love periods, she even understands how she felt when Samyuktha revealed this news that too in front of her lovely giggles. Without a second thought, she ran towards her and hugs tightly. Hansi holds Samyuktha over her left arm. Yash and Parikshith move towards them lean over her shoulders. Michael tears out and moves from them a bit not see her crying a lot meanwhile Lenin, he didn't cry, react, console, and not even moved from the spot. His eyes filled with many sorry witnessing Samyuktha that he made her feels even after her would-be vanished from her memory. When everyone is staying with her, Samyuktha with watery reddish eyes staring at Lenin and raises her hand over him portray that she needed them, this trip, and this moment to share what she holding till now.

From Lenin's point of view no matter how men's behavior of expression appears with women. If women seek to share their thoughts, happy or sad moments, and every bit of seconds with you that not only mean she like a man, she expects last for that man to be with her no matter what happens, how much dark enfolds, even at her last moments she needs you for holding her hands. That's she. A Woman!

That was a huge sad moment for our hues. They even can't pour out the words to console their queen. Imagine how you would feel if your most loved giggle spell out that she lost her lover, or a person who you imagined that your friends will be happy with them had faded off from this universe. Is it so Tragedy, right?

They came from the top view without chatting, having fun, making a smile, and mainly having eye contact. They started went the car and move on to the next spot **Rippon Tea Factory.**

Michael "*I don't want to come with you guys, let me stay in the car!*"

Ayesha "*Okay, you need company?*"

Michael shouts out "*No!*" and begins to control his tears

Lenin in Figo holds the steering and start to think, he had many thoughts running over his mind

"*Why Didn't I shed a bit of tear, do I care for her?*"

"*Or Do I have none of my thoughts for her as my friend!*"

"*How come these people are reacting towards her, Why don't I?*"

"*What If, She was not my friend?*"

"*Then, why do I feel happiness by hanging around them?*"

"*I need to cry now, cry now, cry now, and come on dude!*"

"*Come on dude!, we need to go*" Yash stepped out from the car and calls him.

He stepped and still in an oscillation about his thoughts, with the confusion they reached the factory and visit the factory without any interest. It was like Zombies visiting Disney Land for the first time, no reaction, no expression, they even had freshly made tea from there, but their tasteless and muted face conveyed there were some strange things happened to them.

"*You people are okay?*" A guy who guided the tea factory and serves tea pleased them. "*Yeah, we're all good!*" Ayesha replied.

"*Your faces, not indicating that you're okay!*" he questions back. "*Nothing much!, just a simple thing*" replies came from Samyuktha. "*We, the humans, often worry for past like simple things, that's our nature*"

Yash had a spark over his words and smiles a bit "*Yes, that's our nature*"

Suddenly, all of the hue's vantage point moved towards Yash, "*What made you feel for this, man?*" said Hansi with a jerk.

Yash replied, "*Let me clear you tonight, at our booze times!*"

Beer bottles open with foam which rolled out through the opener. They were assembled for a whole damn debate at the dinner table located inside the tree house.

Michael does not react to what they are chatting, Yash signs to Lenin to kicks start the tech-savvy for hot and spicy debate. He opens slowly with a bit of confused "So, you are relationship goals end here... Right?" points to Samyuktha

Samyuktha "*I am in love with Krishna*"

The whole gang tends to feel a high voltage shock "*What the....*"

Yash in silent mode "*Fuck! Dude*"

Color Splash: Orange

1st June 1:45 AM a Wednesday, Samyuktha was in a rush to complete her research paper. She dressed up as a businesswoman. She was preparing her speech by sitting near the cafeteria in her college

"Completed?" said Krishna. Krishna Kumar, a tall and fit, highly orthodox, resembles Grey from fifty shades of Grey studying in her college, one year senior for Samyuktha.

"No, Kicha I have not yet completed the scenario Mr.Sourav going to screw me" worried Samyuktha

"Mr.Sourav is on leave" Krishna gave a glitch

"What?" Samyuktha questioned with excitement "Why are you excited? He is just on leave that doesn't mean your work is complete. And Ms.Samyuktha you have an extra 24 hrs from your side to complete research. Starting now" Krishna snaps with a smile

"Kicha you making me more anxious about the work" Samyuktha with an awkward face

"Sam, to my knowledge you are not well for the past two weeks. May I know the reason?" questioned Krishna

"Kicha... that was a...." Samyuktha limp in her words. She doubted whether to share it with him or not. She believes Vidya rather than anyone on her campus. Now, she is on an oscillation of whether to trust Krishna and share everything that happens to her.

"No need. For me, you are a brave one who faces everything bold and stands on our decision to make it right. Samyuktha If am I not, try to overcome the past... maybe a worst one to

become who you are" Krishna concerned his point of view.

Samyuktha didn't reply anything yet she was in a double mind state to smile or not for his console.

"Hey! You coming" a pretty voice rose beside Krishna, Jenny Krishna's batchmate calling him

"Yeah I am coming, Think about it Samyuktha!" Krishna pays a good off with a warm console

When Krishna was moving with Jenny she whispers silently "You said?" "No She is fed up with something else Let me deliver in some other good time" Krishna replies

"Krishna!" Samyuktha called him. Jenny silently advises him "Dude! Do you a good time to propose to her?"

Krishna was about to move towards Samyuktha. Before he turns towards Samyuktha he opens up "No, Any time is a good time in my life"

When Krishna comes closer to Samyuktha before she opens up "I am in love with you Sru" Krishna revealed the magic

Samyuktha was shocked and in a statue mode "It doesn't matter what your current situation or past, my love towards you will never make you bored like Mr. Sourav's class I can assure you that. Think along with this too" Krishna with a smile he slowly faded out from Samyuktha's sight

At Present

Michael with anger "*So, you are in love with Krishna!*"

Samyuktha shoots her questions back "*Why not? What is your objection?*"

Yash interfere "*How did you girls accept guys coincide with your taste*"

Ayesha enters now "*How do boys fall in love with a girl?*"

Lenin "*We, either by looks or characters*"

Hansi "*Imagine if a girl proposes to you, will you accept all of a sudden!*"

Michael" *If the girl is already known and if she good enough, then it is, a yes*"

Parikshith" *That's what I did!*"

Lenin "*Every man will, but women?*"

Hansi and Ayesha strike their replies at the same time.

Hansi "*we won't!*"

Ayesha" *Yes, of course*"

The present situation bags three women including an entrepreneur, one yet-to-be a good homemaker, and one typical human. But at the other end, four men, three with a mindset that women wish to grab guys just like accessories and there is no true love beyond women's pathetic eyes, and one committed human being, who is texting to his girl and mostly surrender his opinion completely towards his queen.

Hansi begins her point of view. Hansi states "*She won't unless she completely believe, and also she thinks from her lovable ones point of views*"

Michael "*Yes! Note that, women's brains are specious that it consists of four parts; cerebrum, cerebellum, medulla oblongata, and...*"

Samyuktha questions him "*and?*"

Yash replies "*High-level Empathy*" and gave a loud Hi-fi to Lenin with a laugh

Ayesha who character matches almost 90 % with the anonymous women whom they are mocking can't spare the moment.

Then, Ayesha spoors out her thoughts "*Women will also accept him if he is good and gentle!*"

Lenin interrupts "*Like?*"

Yash replies again "*Men with either good looks or well-settled financial backgrounds, am I right?*"

Michael interrupts "*Hey Chill! Even women had break-up with guys like me, It's happening!*"

Hansi raises her middle finger pointing at him and replies "*Michael... none of the women rejected you, the one who breakups your relationship is you!*"

Michael sarcastically replies "*No women break up without any backup, Guys!*"

Yash "*That's why? Women were blindly believed in arrange marriage*"

Lenin's internal beast unleashes "*Hetero breed Stockholm syndrome victims*"

Ayesha with her base voices "*What? What did you say?*"

Lenin begins "*Have you ever heard of disorder Stockholm syndrome?*"

Samyuktha "*How is that disorder familiar to our situation?*"

Lenin " *It is psychological conditions victims of abuse or kidnap feeling positivity or even falling in with captor. Just imagine Kidnapper as husband and wife as the victims that are the exact thing happening around us. Just like the Stockholm syndrome effect. An Indian Arrange marriage system*"

Ayesha "*Stop it! Lenin, Just...*" Ayesha is typically more sensitive compared to others. Her tears explain that women are not like what he explains but she can't express in her words.

Yash with tears "*Even some of the women applicable to your theory man!*"

The whole plot remains silent and everyone tends to stick with their point. Suddenly the phone rings "*Hey Babe!*" Parikshith responds with a charm to his honey. Our hues turn towards him, like zombies looking on a noninfected human.

Parikshith came out from the spot to shower kisses and pleases to his sweetheart. Now it's three men and women, they don't want to add on any special or even more spies to their conversation. Silently Ayesha moves with tears from the dining room. Where else, Samyuktha move from there to console her. Three men react like they have been staying with unwanted personalities. Hansi pulls over Michael kings and lights it up "*Guys, you want some!*"

Three men knob their heads and move from the place. Hansi stops with cautious advice "*Never let ego drain your love even in disaster, my dear boys!*"Pakrishith returns from the call with one hell of a smile "*I'm back!" Three men shout mutually "We're done!*"

CHAPTER VI

Tint

Edakkal Cave

Trip Day 3, the 14th of June, morning 7:30 AM. The sunrises around the interior of their rooms. Three men were asleep on the living room sofa. Lenin woke up slowly and saw two monsters next to him, Michael over his shoulder and Yash on his lap. He rubs at his eyes to see clearly and stands up, Sam and Ayesha were looking at him, sitting on the loft, they seemed all ready for the next location.

"*Hansi?*" Lenin questions them. Sam points to the opened front door, immediately Lenin moves from the sofa, waking up those two creatures all the while adjusting his loose shorts. Hansi was checking the car's condition and getting it set for a long drive. "*Hey Hippi! You woke up!*" he nodded his head slowly and began to voice his doubt, "*Do they still-*""*-Yes, they are still fighting*" she replied "*Well I am too!*" he argued.

"*What's your problem?*" She asked, sitting on the car's (Figo) hood. "*I admit zero anger towards them; I only worry about their mindset!*" "*Mindset? What do you mean about it?*" she stared at him.

"*The way women see men, are we just accessories to you? Sometimes, I just wonder why women choose men and spend a lot of time with them, just to leave them behind with no thought?*" he says, controlling his tears. "*Who's she?*" Hansi questions knowingly. "*Who are you asking about?*" He questioned back. "*The Woman, who didn't left you!*"

"She is..." Lenin starts softly. Suddenly *"Just shut up, don't touch me!"* Ayesha shouts out loud. *"Michael?"* Hansi voices out her doubt. *"It's our rock star!"* They both rushed inside the house and straight into the mess. Yash is trying to share his thoughts to Ayesha who is not willing to enter into any sort of conversation with him.

Hansi got a hold on Granny, meanwhile Lenin held Yash *"Guys, please stop."* Hansi begs. They both huff in frustration and walk off in opposite directions. Ayesha slowly moves to the washbasin with her toothbrush. When she begins to squeeze her paste *"For me?"* another hand with a toothbrush butts in. She looks up at the culprit and argues *"I won't forgive-"* Michael interrupts *''Forgive who?"* and the cold war continues.

By 9:00 AM, Both the cars were wheeling out into the road against the shining sun rays on the hills. It made a pleasant morning as a good start for apologies, wishes, fun and deep thoughts about each other.

Since it was a weekday and they started at work time; the place they planned to go to had very few tourists other than our hues. That place being Edakkal cave, which means a large rock stocked in between two hills. The Figo and Swift are parked before the entrance and they have to walk a bit over the hills to the ticket counter, which is the entry point of the cave. From the Swift three girls rolled out and the boys from the Figo. They were very frustrated because of the morning food, because yes, they missed breakfast in order to get here faster.

The girls moved faster, wanting to stay away from the boys. The three single ones and the only one committed with a phone, struggling for signal, were sailing slowly along the hills like a powered down vehicle. Way ahead of everyone Hansi begins *"Why can't you girls forget it?"* Ayesha sighs *"See, three things; first of all, I don't want to talk about this!"*

Samyuktha interrupts *"Hansi, leave her. What would you do if someone touched your ego and laughed at you?"*

Hansi *"Just a minute! Let her finish!"*

Ayesha *"What do I have to finish?"* They were moving slowly to have a clear conversation.

Hansi questions back *"Your second and third things?"*

Ayesha *"Second, You know about his personality right?"*

Hansi replies *"Yeah! Point. The third one?"*

Ayesha raises her eyebrows *"Well! Who am I to forgive them?"*

Hansi puts a dot in one word reply *"Friend"*

Hansi continues *"They are your one little family, one good companion. You know this morning he came to you to apologize not to hurt you. Hey! Do you remember? In our college, you keep on saying this; our friends will never leave us even when we hurt them. Why can't we do that back? Granny, you are one good soul in every relation you have. We can't hold a grudge towards them. But we can understand their situation and forgive them, right?"*

Samyuktha hesitates *"Situation?"*

Hansi *"Lenin's love life has failed and Yash's too."*

Samyuktha stands stunned for a while and turns towards them. The three of them were climbing and playing with each other with a pack of smiles on their cheeks *"Did Lenin fall in love with a girl?"* Hansi replies *"Yes!"*

When they reached the ticket counter, Hansi turned back and shouted *"Guys!"* she pointed over to a shop where they can get Kerala special Bamboo rice Payasam*

(Payasam: It is a pleasant and sweet dessert, not even the south Indians can resist)

All of them rushed towards the shop like Spartans and ordered two glasses of payasam each. When the boys began to fill their tummies Yash turned towards Ayesha and nudged his filled glass to her, apologizing in a friendly way "*For you!*"

Ayesha smiles back and accepts his offer "*Why can't you smile for a change? You Moron*"

After a while they each took another round of Payasam each for their empty stomachs leading the store to run out of it pretty soon. Samyuktha holds the last glass and sees Lenin licking his own that has few drops leftover. She grabs his glass and fills it with what she had and yells "*Cheers!*"

Lenin smiled back and replied "*Cheers!*"

After the sweet apology, they bought tickets for Edakkal cave and moved inside the dense forest where they scaled steps that lead to explore the beauty of Edakkal. From the foot of the stairs, Ayesha moves closer to Lenin accompanying him for his photography, the rest of the colors shatter all throughout the cave.

Ayesha holds Lenin's left arm tighter and moves forward on the stairs slowly. Meanwhile he is setting the ISO in his camera for capturing the seismic beauty of the cave. She doesn't want to hurt him by making him remember the past and bury him with her own memories. She can't resist holding her concerns for too long though so she burst out "*Who's she?*" "*Haya. Haya Marium, my classmate*" he smiled back.

Ayesha sees that he's blushing and points it out "*Hey man! I have never seen you like this.*" She raises her hands to hold his cheeks and he immediately stops smiling, going silent.

Ayesha questions "*What happened, Hippi? Will you share what's in your clumsy mind?*"

Color Splash: Red

When Haya called Lenin for a coffee break, they went off to the nearest café located facing their college parking slot. The café is on the ground floor of the building with two double seaters in the open balcony, the interiors designed with Barbie dolls, Power puff girls and Captain Marvel posters. Especially the takeaway counter with coffee flavoured stickers

They reached the café and Haya placed her notes on the table located in one of the double seaters in the balcony. Lenin, in a rush to impress her exclaims "Ah! That's my favourite spot too!"

Haya replies back "Lenin, I haven't said this is my favourite spot. Just to relax myself, I kept my stuff here."

Lenin manages a shy uncomfortable smile "Thought that we both have the same taste. Leave it Haya, What shall I order for you?"

Haya questions with a hunched back "We both have the same taste, right? You go order my favourite and yours too! Let's see the result."

Lenin walks towards the counter, takes out his mobile and begins his cyber stalking. Wait a minute! There are around 3.6 billion social media users, in Facebook approximately 2.7 billion users were scrolling up and down, uploading, commenting, harassing, protesting, stalking, chatting, and undergoing many things. But there are some meta humans in this same inbound marketers filled world who don't need to post, publish, and establish their interest and internal thoughts to others. Unfortunately Haya is one of those so-called meta humans.

Lenin moves closer to the counter, he ponders for a while and figures out Haya's favourite dessert. His internal talks cheer him up "Dude! She is a bold and brisk woman, so order a wine cake." On the other end of his brain something chimed in "Wait wait! She is a studious girl too. What if she likes cappuccino?" Now, he thinks deeper and talks to himself "Wine cake or Cappuccino, this or that! What else! Come on, Lenin!"

"One hot coffee please!" Haya interrupts and questions "For you?"

"Wine ca-oh sorry! Same hot coffee for me!" He replies back.

They both strangled each other with looks until the ordered coffee was being prepared. Lenin admired her straightforward attitude, her polite tone and her self- confident words made her look even more admirable.

Waitress places their coffee at the counter and calls out, "Your coffee, Ma'am!"

Lenin goes to pick it up and takes three packs of white sugars. He turns towards her "Sugar?"

"I don't add white sugar, Lenin!" She takes her coffee and moves outside.

She sits on the coffee table facing the road and drags the opposite chair for him.

Lenin starts slowly "Haya, I have doubts in EI"

Haya casually shoots her question "Topic?"

Lenin figures that she is purposefully testing him. He is well prepared though to maintain the debate "Interpersonal relationships."

Haya opens up her notes and starts to describe the topic from her own understanding. "Basically, interpersonal relationships are social relations, affiliations or connections between two peoples."

Lenin interrupts her "Like us!"

Haya, doesn't focus on the guy's flirting words, "Yeah, we could be an example. Like us!" She continues her lecture, "Non verbal communications is an important factor in interpersonal communications where one should exhibit right tone and facial expressions, and even fake expressions can be easily found out!"

While she demonstrates seriously through her words, Lenin falls into Haya mode that makes her words become poetry. She keeps her eyes on the notes and she doesn't even feel romantic vibes with what he does. Suddenly, she stops and lightly slaps Lenin's cheeks "Concentrate!"

Lenin paused his activity and said "What? Where did we leave off?"

Haya replied "From the beginning!"

Lenin justifies "Sorry Haya, I literally felt compelled to stare at you!"

Haya asks shocked, "What?"

Lenin replies "No! I witnessed slight differences in your tone!"

Haya closes the notes and starts to lecture about interpersonal communications practically with him "Lenin, have you gone through the topic anytime?"

Lenin smiles "No, You are my first teacher."

Haya spells out "If you were, then you'll be able to stalk even better."

Lenin "Is it so?"

Haya "Stop it Buddy! Today you presented a demo in our class right?"

Lenin starts with joy "Yes, Yes! About Empathy."

Haya "Then, measure my thoughts, face expressions and behaviour and estimate how I should be communicated with?"

Lenin opens up "I love you, Haya!"

Haya was stunned by his words but she doesn't give a damn, she slowly starts to address her situation "Lenin, May I know what made you say this?"

Lenin replies "My internal talks, one gut feeling!"

Haya questions back "Lenin, Just imagine, if you were born as a woman in a family where men tend to hold women aside their wishes, and still permit to let her go where she wants with the one agreement, to marry a man who they point at, and never accomplish any dreams without their permission."

Lenin switched to silent mode and dropped his head down. Haya held his face and said "Chin up, Lenin! It's not your fault. You are among the men I know. You also will expect these things from your daughter, right? We women have desires too. But we usually focus on relationships along with our dreams. I couldn't consider your proposal because you can't be with me until the end of the line. We cannot!"

She slowly wiped her tears and said "Lenin, work towards your vision, not for your fantasies. I am sure that you will succeed in your life above your expectations, I believe you and I know that you are a one good interpersonal communicator buddy!" With all her words she ruffled his yet-to-be-bald hair and saw her watch, "Oh it's time! I need to go. Okay see you buddy, and thanks for heeding my advice."

When Haya moves from the table, Lenin holds her left hand and questions her "So, it's a no, right?"

Haya replied with a gentle look "I am committed, Lenin!"

At Present

Ayesha shouts "*What? No way!*"

Lenin replies "*That's the end. she faded away!*"

Ayesha said "*Oh! This is the reason for your scary words last night. Now I understand the whole thing.*"

Ayesha eagerly asks "*Who is he? I mean her boyfriend!*"

Lenin puts a full stop "*No Ayesha, please, I don't want to talk about it. I came to this trip to forget about that but whenever we argue; it's reminding me of Haya!*"

Ayesha questions, "*How come she and our friends resemble each other? Is she so beautiful?*"

Lenin laughs for a second and replies back "*No! She is prettier than anybody else. But you both have the same mindset, never letting go of your dreams. You both tried to focus on your relationships along with your dreams.*"

Ayesha from her end asks "*Is that wrong?*" Lenin keeps silent as he can't debate with her words.

Ayesha holds his hand and says "*We women usually wish to hold every soul we love. We want everyone to be with us but unfortunately whatever we dream, it will fade out as a dream. In that case, Men are very lucky, right?*"

Lenin realizes his mistakes and friendship towards her. He holds her hand in between stairs inside a complete dense part, bird's song, insects whispering and trees tickling through the breezy air, he can hear her heart pound calmly. There is a Buddhist's quote, 'When you meet your soul mate you'll feel calm. No anxiety, no agitation.' It's applicable for friendship too. Ayesha is someone like that but he is afraid to say anything that could hurt her again. Lenin slowly tries to console her with soft words and soothing sounds.

He turns her head forward and she witnesses a calm scene, a greenery look, and breathes in the fresh air. Both of them reached the center of the cave, a soft place where every color looked so bright and smiled at each other by holding each other's hands. They formed a circle like a cricket team before they went in to bowl. "*Shall we begin?*" Samyuktha raises her eyebrows.

"*Oh yeah!*" Parikshith replies and all of sudden, they all begin to scream "*Hurray!*"

CHAPTER VII

Black & White

Venue: Bird Sanctuary

Sun kisses the dark forest at noon, our hues enter a location of 344.44 sq. km filled with miracles of all kinds including mammals, birds, reptiles, amphibians and fishes where temperature varies between 13°C to 32°C. Every colour looking towards our beloved Lenin, his face filled with so much brightness that made their time feel more precious. Even though he had six good looking people beside him, his intentions were to shoot the wildlife inside the sanctuary.

They entered the forest with the help of a forest guide in a green colored Mahindra THAR. Michael was placed in the front seat, remaining colors all settled, facing each other in the back seat of the truck. When Lenin turns towards the outside and sees through his 50mm lens, beginning to explore nature, a completely different creature catches him from behind.

"*Hey! Happy?*" Samyuktha climbed over him, "*You know I accepted this trip mainly to capture these creatures!*" His excitement stays turned up.

Suddenly the whole gang giggles and Yash pulls over the camera and questions "*Why can't you click your pals?*" All the while placing his camera holding hand on Ayesha's shoulder.

They realise that they had reunited after a massive cold war from the previous night when they smile at each other. Yash takes her hand in his own and says "*Sorry!*" Ayesha stares back and pulls his hand back to place it over her shoulder and argues "*It's a punishment. Never leave me alone!*"

Whole gang shouts out loud "Oh!" Yash blushes and moves from his seat to sit near Samyuktha.

Now Ayesha, Parikshith and Hansi were on one side and Samyuktha, Yash and the photography addict settled on the other end. Samyuktha looks at Yash and starts the interrogation "*What made you yell last night?*"

Yash slowly opens up about his secret, "*She was my colleague and slowly she became my girlfriend, but now, she is my ex.*" Samyuktha seemed shocked, "*Oh!*"

"*She is Renukha; a polite, gentle and agoraphobic woman. At 22, she was scared even to cross the road. When we first met, I didn't have that much empathy towards her. She cried every time I got angry. So I had to control my anger to stop her tears and make her smile. When she proposed to me, her eyes were filled with tears that clearly stated her fear of rejection? I accepted the proposal not only because of her innocence but also for the way she treated me. I didn't even know people were divided by certain cultural rules at the time we loved each other. They even look around for a lover using only those rules. Fuck our ancestors, man! I had no idea what happened for the last two months. My life has become a puzzle because of the irrelevant protocols written so long ago. Why do we live based on their wishes? We resemble robots functioning with only the manual programmed by them. Regardless of it all, fate played a role too. I never expected to live through all the transformations of a woman in my life; a stranger, a teammate, a friend, a girlfriend, a good soul, my dream-girl, a well wisher and now a stranger again. She is my ex now.*"

"*Fuck man!*" Hansi interferes. "*There is no such term as ex. Did she tell you she didn't like you?*"

"*No.*" Yash replied.

"Did she say she won't love you anymore?" shoots again.

"No."

"Did she say she hates you?" shoots one again.

"No."

"Then, she is not your ex man. Cheer up!" Hansi holds his hand and motivates him from her end.

"Hey Hansi, wait a minute! Did she get married?" Ayesha questions in a softer tone.

Yash had no replies to that, yet his left eye tearing up revealed the answer as *"Yes!"*

Ayesha holds his hands tight and advises *"It's okay. Yash? It's okay to leave someone to live your own life. I may not share your feelings but can I share your tears?"* Yash suddenly looks at her face. Tears rolled down her eyes too.

"Hey! Don't. I am not worried for her." He wiped her tears, held her shoulders and answered back holding her arms. *"My only guilt was that I should not have yelled at you, saying what was in my mind seemed right only in that moment. Sorry for that, Ayesha."*

Ayesha slowly releases herself from his hands and slaps back with a sweet reply *"Don't say words like that, especially to me, to us. Don't ever compare us with anyone who leaves you either, okay?"*

Yash knocks their heads together with a mixture of tears and smiles.

"Who is she to leave you? Say that you left her to live your own life, because you are always our hero, Yash!" Ayesha argues from the bottom of her heart.

Yash puts his head down and wipes his tears; *"Yash, heads up man! A hero should never put his head down!"* Ayesha consoles and continues *"Mr. Perfect, Look here!"*

"Guys! Look what I've found, a spotted deer!" Lenin turns back and shows his DSLR.

At that moment, they realized that while everyone else was in a sentimental mood, only one imposter from the group wore a Bluetooth headset and was busy with his wildlife photography.

"*An impassive creature spotted inside the truck*" Parikshith replies hilariously.

When Lenin figured that something went down while he was busy with his stuff, he too opened up his thoughts on it to show mutual understanding. "*It's not that serious, It happens most of the time. Even Michael broke up with Aishu. He manages well enough, right?*"

The whole story moved from Yash to Michael. Parikshith slowly grabs Michael's collar and questions "*So, you still haven't changed?*"

Samyuktha shakes hands with Lenin, pleased "*Thanks for your cooperation, Michael's boy bestie*!"

Michael argues "*What? Do you people need to know my past now?*"

Hansi "*When will you be done with your flirting era?*"

When she shoots his inquiry their safari ride ends in a place nearer to a large banyan tree located beside a tea stall. Our Colors had a tea break with some warm Kerala crispy snacks. Both Lenin and Michael took a smoke break and remained seated over the wooden bench in the tea stall. Michael turns towards Hansi and says, "*Is it necessary to be in love with a woman in my teenage years or do we just need an opposite gender companion to hangout and share good times with. No! Then what else do we need? I am fed up with relationships, now I've broken up with Aishu a number of times. But, I don't know why? She still holds onto me, never gives up, she stands by me at any cost, anytime, any situation. Yash, I sometimes feel jealous of you. What if I replace your past with mine? And you girls! why are you so nice to the person who you fall in love with, even after breaking up?"*

Ayesha answers his questions "*You moron! That's love, a pure woman's love!*" Parikshith interrupts with his pre-wedding thoughts "*Try to enjoy your bachelorhood friends before you commit; once you enter the hell, you are completely screwed, man!*"

Their bird sanctuary kick-starts with fun, even though they went through emotional rides they eventually end back at the absurdity of it all. Michael loves his friend more than anyone in his life, which explains that although he slips up with his girlfriends, he never misses spending time with his friends.

CHAPTER VIII

Brightness

Karlad Lake

It's Day 3, the 14th of June around 3 o'clock noon. The next location specially intended for the adventure lover Parikshith , who loves to be thrilled more than anything. Wayanad is famous for its adventurous location as well as south India's longest zip line across the lake. Just 10 acres of land, mainly built for activities like kayaking, rock climbing, and boating. Located 15km away from Wayanad's center is the magnificent Karlad Lake.

"Babe! I won't be available for the next three hours, it's my time to celebrate the trip!" said Parikshith to his would-be as if it's an announcement. They went to the ticket counter and looked at the menu for adventure sports. *"Zip line!"* Samyuktha says and Parikshith gives her a Hi-fi. In no time, they both were moving for the zip line excitedly. Hansi and Ayesha dragged Yash towards them and requested *"Bony, we need to talk a lot so please come boating with us."*

"Dude, I have two more Dunhill!" Michael gestures to Lenin. *"Should we get outside of the park then?"* Lenin questions back.

"Nope, have you smoked in the middle of a lake before?" Michael asks Lenin with a wink.

"No! No, don't you dare Mich-" Lenin begins to refuse but Michael pulls him towards the Kayaking spot even though Lenin was extremely scared of water.

Starting here, Along with Hues timeline moves in a non-linear where perspective, thoughts, risks, lives, even deaths interferes at one point.

Boating

"*So, what do you think?*" Ayesha questions Yash.

Yash replied "*What do you mean?*"

Hansi "*Will you meet her again?*"

"*No way!*" replies Yash as he turns back.

Hansi again strikes back "*Seriously Bonny !*"

Yash "*Why would I want to see her again?*"

Hansi "*Would she think the same, you fool?*"

Yash's voice double downs "*She-.*" He thinks about it and replies with a straightforward answer "*No!*"

Hansi "*Oh my god, Yash. Why won't you speak up when it comes to this?*"

Ayesha "*Because she still is important to him.*"

Yash "*Guys, what would you do if you were in my situation?*"

Ayesha "*I don't even need a boyfriend!*"

Meanwhile the both of them turn towards Hansi and whisper theatrically "What if she does!"

Hansi stops them both and begins "Wait, let me explain what happened?"

Color Splash: Purple

Noon came; Hansi was searching for the resort using the coupon codes generated on the vacation website. She was considering Ooty in terms of flexibility in capacity. She gets hung up on the one thing that sparks her interest, that's why she can't focus on any of the other places. She clicks the location as India. Many places showed up so she scrolled faster by searching for peaceful places where they can even stargaze undisturbed. A particular location stops her like a red signal. A place blanketed with nature, completely covered behind mist, in a country that's dubbed as God's own - Wayanad. She moves over to the images and is immediately fascinated by the inherent beauty. Just as she clicks on the **Book** *option, a sudden mail icon pings at the bottom right corner of her system.*

A Business requisition mail received with complex task briefing and that which requires her to be present for the upcoming 3 months.

Dear Hansi,

Please work on the following project for the upcoming three months.

Regards,

Ankit

Hansi opened the mail for project briefing; they seemed to be a year's worth of tasks scheduled to be completed within the next three or four months. Hansi was literally fed up and realized that she cannot join the trip. She thought about skipping the project in order to be with her favourite idiots. So she turned to Ankit's cabin and raised her seat a bit higher to check whether he was there.

Ankit was busy on a call. "Busy bee" a man's voice silently pulled her away from Ankit. Next to Hansi's cubicle Shiva spoke with raised eyebrows, "So, you are going to drive the project forward, right?"

"How did you know that?" Hansi wondered.

"Because, I am the one who suggested this to Ankit; to involve you in this project." Shiva laughed cunningly.

"Shiva, why? What did I do to you? I have my personal issues to take care of in the upcoming weeks." Hansi hides her

vacation plan.

"I know what the personal issue is. It's about your friends and your trip, right?" Shiva replied.

Hansi raised her voice while fuming with anger "You were snooping on my regular activities?"

Shiva "Hey It's all cool! That's what every boy does when they fall in love with a girl. What is wrong with that?" replied with a smile.

Hansi "You know, Shiva, this is not love. And this isn't the way to impress a girl!"

Shiva begins, with a no-good smile on his face "You don't need to get angry. Instead you need to be thinking about what you need to do to get over this situation."

Hansi stands up from her chair "Okay Mr. Perfect, provide me with a valuable solution for this current bug."

Shiva "You have only two options. One, you can take over the project and perform throughout the complete timeline. Two, you can accept my proposal!"

Hansi "What is the profit in accepting your proposal, Shiva?"

Shiva "That's my trick. If you accept my proposal, I will take over the project for you, then you can enjoy your vacation with your beloved friends."

Hansi "Do you have any idea about what you are talking about? This is not fair, Shiva."

Shiva replies "Everything is fair in love and war, Hansi"

Hansi stalls Shiva for a few seconds and then casually opens her table drawer and takes an Esse. Shiva's cunning face instantly turns tense and he can already feel the upcoming response from Hansi.

She turned towards Ankit and saw that he was out of his cabin, moving closer to them.

Hansi shouts from her own cubicle, "Ankit, would you like to join me for a smoke, I need to discuss a few things about the new project."

Ankit waves his hands to keep it quiet "Shh! Okay sure, I am coming Ms. Hansi. Why do you need to say it with such arrogance?"

They both move towards the smoking zone on their floor. She turns just in time to see Shiva's angry face spelling out "Shit!"

"That's exactly what your idea is. Fuck you!" Hansi smiles and gives him the middle finger with pride.

At Present

Yash shivered like he had a high voltage of shock passing through him.

Ayesha suddenly interrupts "*Then, how did you manage to come with us!*"

Hansi replied "*Simple, I quit my job!*"

Ayesha Hugs Hansi "*That's awesome!*" Yash stills at Hansi's reply.

Hansi raises her eyebrows at Yash questioningly, still hugging Ayesha.

Yash, still shocked out of his mind, whispers "*You are a freaking Maleficent*!"

At this point, Ayesha and Hansi were hugging each other at the edge of the boat while Yash sat facing them. Behind their boat, Ayesha could see Michael and Lenin kayaking. She spots the oddness of it before anyone else and within a fraction of a second she sees the movement and shouts "*No! Lenin!*"

When the three of them turn back, they watch Lenin, who had no swimming experience whatsoever dive into the lake.

Kayaking

15 minutes earlier

Michael and Lenin were getting ready for Kayaking in front of the anchored boat, as well as the ride down their nostalgia.

"*Damn, you won't leave me even if you are going to hell, huh*?" scolds Lenin.

Michael smiles and secures Lenin's life jacket, "*If you're going through hell, keep going, my friend!*"

"*Fuck you, man!*" said Lenin, exasperated.

When Michael steps inside the boat, Lenin's pupils shake and his body arrests in fear. Michael grabs his hands to pull him down onto the kayak, "*It's nothing, dude! It's just a stupid sport, see!*"

Michael settled in the front while Lenin cowers on the back seat. The boat starts and in no time they're sailing.

Michael orders "*Dude! See that curve? That dense forest. That's our destination. You see it?*"

Lenin replies "*Only my grave is visible to me, you dumbass!*"

"*Why do you keep on babbling like a woman?*" Michael sounds and shakes the boat teasingly.

"*Hey, watch it man! I was just kidding okay? By the way, how can you say that!?*" The question comes from Lenin's heart.

"*Say what?*" Michael

"'*Blabber like a woman' Have you not gone through anything? You've never seen men complain about their lives?*" Lenin

"No! You are the first guy who's ever talked like this." smiles Michael.

Lenin smiles back and begins his internal talks *"You broke up with many women and all they did was complain about their situation. That's why you hate that, right?"*

Michael *"Yes, once I reject a proposal or we break up, they start to complain and cry. I don't know why they feel the need to keep on holding on to a man, even when they wish to move on from them."*

Lenin explains *"Because they all thought that you were the only one who would hold onto them in their toughest times. But when you suddenly change things upside down, it'll be hard for them to can't accept it, dude!"*

Michael *"That's why I am asking. Just why? Why do they behave like that?"*

Lenin explains it all with kind words from his own experiences, *"Because, they never want to hurt you back. They don't even hold vengeance against the men who make them cry."*

Michael *"That's why I hate those women who are too emotional."*

Lenin replies *"Women are emotionally intelligent by birth, my friend!"*

While Lenin pours out some words from his own internal wounds, a weird cigarette smoke comes from the front end of the boat *"Fuck! Mick, what are you doing?"*

"Don't worry, I've got one for you too!" he replied

In the middle of kayaking, these two youngsters have a smoke break right between the water, surrounded by the wild forest. *"That's great, let me get a taste then,"* Lenin smiled back.

Michael laughs and gives Lenin's share. They turn the boat around to return to the spot where they began.

Michael "*Dude, I wonder about this many times.*"

Lenin after a smooth puff "*What about?*"

Michael "*What if you were in my situation? Will you go ahead with the break-up or suffer in silence?*"

Lenin's mind voice echoed "*I am already suffering man!*"

"*I wish to be like you sometimes. How come you can behave so casually? I mean you broke up recently, right?*" He questioned him.

And just in time, the kayak reached the place where they started and Michael answered it himself.

Michael "*Dude, Everything is love in this universe. Nothing more, nothing less. Everyone has their own person caring for them. No matter what you do, good or bad or nothing, there will be someone to stand along with you and that is love. But we wish to have an opposite gender companion to share and control and get controlled. Sometimes we show off that we have a good girl or boy as a spouse. So, there is no reason to get worried. Just sit back and chill, you'll be showered with love in each and every second.*"

Lenin smiles back "*Did she have the same idea as you? What if she got stuck in your memories?*"

"*Will she?*" he hesitated.

"*Have you ever asked her?*" Lenin punches back.

"*No, dude! She may get offended and sensitive too!*" Michael

"*That's love, man. She loves you,*" Lenin smiles and crushes his smoke and secures it in a cover.

Michael remains silent without any replies. Lenin uses this silence "So, *was it?*"

Lenin "*Promise me, that you'll never leave her!*"

Michael "*Just shut up, man! Are you going to die the next minute or something to keep up a promise with you?*"

Lenin laughs and continues "*Dude, you are the one acting like a philosopher and a debater at the same time!*"

Michael and Lenin parked the boat and began to remove the life jackets. Lenin was standing away from the wood and Michael was at the edge of the wooden bench to tie the boat.

Michael "*If I need to promise, then you should do one thing for me.*"

When he completes the words and turns back, he sees Lenin rushing to dive into the lake without his life jacket on, shouting "*Sam!*"

Zip Line

30 minutes earlier

Parikshith and Samyuktha reached the top of the zipline counter. Parikshith seems a little bit frightened but Samyuktha on the other hand has been very excited to zoom over the mountain. He began to clear his doubts away.

Parikshith "*Hey, are you sure you want to try this?*"

Samyuktha "*You'll be with me, right?*"

Parikshith smiles back, "*Nah! I still have to live my life out with my girlfriend!*"

Samyuktha smiles and walks up to the queue; Samyuktha turns back and "*Why are you not mad at me at all?*" she questioned.

"*For what? Krishna?*" He replied.

"*Yes, most of our monsters seemed unhappy when I revealed the news but not you. Why?*" Samyuktha.

"*Because it's you. I can't bear to see you struggling. But when you said that you've restarted your life, I felt like you wanted us to feel the same way. I feared that I'd behave like an ordinary man and not as your friend. But whatever happened has happened. You go ahead, I'll hold you, and I'll stand with you, for sure."* he waved his hands.

Samyuktha hugs him and starts to cry for a bit, she murmurs a thankful reply *"I don't have money to throw a treat for this restart, okay?"*

Parikshith *"Please let me go. You are next, idiot!"*

Samyuktha goes on to tie the rope and takes care of the safety measures. She turns around, shaking her hands off and a long breath in. While Parikshith remembers to ask "*You swim?*"

Samyuktha, "*You forgot that I am a state level swimmer?*"

Trainer, "*Okay ma'am, on my count!*"

He pulls her back and swings her towards the lake. When she starts to move from the top of the mountain, she feels the fresh air, the greenery that's spread around. The warm rays of sun covers her whole, making her realise that her dark and cloud-filled past has broken away to pave her a brand new way.

She still felt thrilled until she undid her rope and fell down the lake.

Freeze! Now, one quick recap over the sequences and expect the unexpected.

Dilemma

Lenin forgot that Samyuktha swims better than a trained swimmer. And even she knows only a complete moron would dive into the freezing lake with no life jacket on.

Each color intertwined with each other to become a dark red with heightened emotion.

Yash, Ayesha and Hansi were in the boat. Michael was on the shore, and Samyuktha swam to the surface to survive while Lenin drowned inside the lake. All of sudden, Parikshith slides down and runs fast as he could to the lake. Until this second, Lenin, inside the lake, experiences a whole lot of things that made him realize that love, friendship, maturity, and moreover the faces he remembers until the end of life.

"Death ends life, not relationships."

Parikshith came across the lake and was searching for the exact point where Lenin fell, since he needed to dive from the opposite side of the shore. Michael shouts out "*To your right!*"

Parikshith takes a few steps backwards and dives into the lake. When he swam deeper and found Lenin half dead, he cried out and broke out of water to drag him to the shore. Where all the colours were struggling and screaming his name. The life support team in the lake moves closer and provides emergency medication.

The team got to work immediately, pumping his chest to restart his heart all the while Samyuktha experiences the same feelings Lenin had towards her in Chemperum peak. She stood still and kept uttering his name again and again.

Michael whispered silently "*Dude, I promise you whatever you want. Please come back!*"

When they realized that they could save him with a bit more effort, Ayesha rubbed his feet to warmth and Hansi held his hand. Within a few seconds of their hard work and desperate pleading, Lenin spat out the water that was filled in his lungs, making it difficult to breathe.

Parikshith sighed and sat down next to him. Lenin opened his eyes "*Dude! Thank-*"

He interrupted with a light slap to Lenin and hugged him with all the love he could muster. Everyone wipe out their own tears and moved closer to join the hug. They held each other tightly and just let their love comfort themselves.

When they held Lenin, he slowly opened his watery eyes again and looked up at the Wayanad hills, covered in all sorts of colors in harmony. He smiles and feels the joy and freedom and mainly unsaid love that they all haven't expressed. But they still felt it during his almost death bed moment. Every human experiences such moments with friends who haven't spilled out some lovely words towards you. They may not show it when you shine your brightest but maybe when you cry in the darkness. They are your colors, your friends for life.

CHAPTER IX

Vivid

The night after the dangerous scuba diving Lenin had, a longer night awaited him. He kept trying to sleep in different positions to make himself comfortable. The remaining colours were discussing their past life and ever-changing hidden feelings they had about each other.

Lenin was on the bed facing the main door, while Hansi and Ayesha sat on the ground, Yash and Michael on the sofa holding a beer, Parikshith leaning against the main door and Samyuktha sat on the table placed in the hall. Lenin was half-sleep, vaguely listening in on their conversation.

Yash yelled *"I haven't ever thought about her side of things post break-up!"*

Ayesha *"Wow, look who's come all this way after a long struggle, our bonny!"*

Parikshith opens up slowly *"Never mind that, dude. I didn't know that this idiot would dive into the lake!"*. Michael opens up the hurt locker*"It's for you, Sam"*

Samyuktha said *"But he hasn't even come near me after the incident at Chemperum peak."*

Hansi *"Yeah, he didn't come to console you. I was shocked why he stayed still like a statue at that time too."*

Yash *"Well, you behaved exactly like him today!"*

Samyuktha had felt the same shockwave Lenin felt at the Chemperum peak. It doesn't matter what the tragedy is, both of them reacted as if they had lost their loved one and were only left with an incurable scar of trauma.

Ayesha *"He came to this trip only for us! To be with us."*

Samyuktha *"What made him accept this trip?"*

Ayesha spit out her name "*A male-dominant mindset, he proposed his classmate!*"

Samyuktha "*Did she really reject our Hippi?*"

Ayesha explained to everyone what he experienced at the Edakkal caves.

Everyone was astonished that the guys who was the clown of their group and made others laugh, could hold intangible tears and hide them just to see his loved ones smile. At this moment Samyuktha realised the reason for Lenin's freeze-over in Chemperum peak. Starting now there are only two plots that run over the story, holding as central point and remaining as subsidiaries; one is Sam's love life, second Lenin's hidden love story

Trip Day 4 rolls around. The 15th of June 8:00 AM in the morning. It started blissfully, the sun making a golden arc over the beautiful mountains of Wayanad. Everyone was busy packing their belongings, softly smiling and hugging each other - a goodbye made of bittersweet tears.

Ayesha, Hansi, Yash, Parikshith and Michael settled themselves in the Figo to be dropped at Koramangala. The Swift was for Lenin and Samyuktha to go to the electronic city.

When they started to leave the place, Parikshith called over Samyuktha "Hey, not just me but we will be with you no matter what happens!"

Samyuktha hugs him and her cheeks turn red with a content smile.

Before Lenin could walk into his car Ayesha called out "*Hey guys, give me a second.*" She broke away from her group and walked down towards Lenin, who was still standing outside his vehicle.

"*She is pretty unlucky to not hold onto our Hippi. But I do realise how much luckier we are to have you here, with your heart as whole as it can be.*" She swayed him left and right softly, holding his cheeks. Michael says from the other end, "*Lenin, I promise to help you with whatever you want.*"

Lenin "*So you remembered the bet?*"

Michael replied "*Of course, you idiot! Since I've lost the bet, what do you want me to do?*"

Lenin smiles and replies "*Marry her!*"

Michael with eye brows raised "*Seriously?*"

He replied "*I'm jealous now! Just marry her idiot, that's my order!*"

Michael and Lenin greet each other with a smile and a hug.

Our Hues all go their own way from here with warmth still clinging onto them.

Secrets on the Highway

"Hey! Wake up, Sam!" Lenin's voice blares like an alarm for her.

"Did we reach already? What's the time?" Samyuktha slowly opens her eyes and regains consciousness.

"No, It's just 2:00 PM. We've covered some decent distance. I thought we could have a pit stop. Do you want to get coffee?" he asked.

"CCD? Yes!" Samyuktha opened her door and rushed inside the coffee shop.

A coffee shop built on the highway where couples can go for long drives and still stop by for coffee with their loved ones. The shop had two floors where they could have a nice view of the highway and some privacy too.

Lenin felt Déjà vu as he stepped into the restaurant. It felt an awful lot like the place he went with Haya. He slowly stepped back and restrained himself from reliving what happened to him, "Not again, no!" he whispered to himself.

"And for you?" Samyuktha asked.

"Whatever you ordered, make it two!" he replied with a frightened face.

"What's the matter? Are you alright?" Samyuktha shook his head slightly, to get his attention.

"Two hot coffees, please!" she ordered hastily. *"It's happening again!"* he could feel the bad feeling rising up inside again. He slowly moved towards the staircase. *"Oh! You like this spot, Hippi?"* She got their orders and sat with him in the open space on the first floor. She silently took in the highway view of the coffee shop.

"Come- Why are you so dumbstruck all of a sudden, dude?" she questioned, worrying about him.

"No, I am not!" he replied. *"Still in Haya mode?"* she winked and had a sip of her coffee.

All of a sudden, Lenin sat straight up on the sofa like he was electrocuted.

"How do you know about Haya?"

Lenin hung his head down for a while. She held his chin and said *"Chin up, Lenin!"* just like Haya. *"I came here with you guys to forget that past. So I hope you understand"* he said so quietly that Samyuktha barely caught his words.

"Forget what? Why, Hippi?" she questioned with another sip from her coffee mug.

"Because I am a loser. I can't even-" he began to explain his side of things. All of a sudden, she gave a light slap to snap him out of it.

"Loser? Fuck you, man! You don't know your worth. You haven't spilled out the story or cursed her out. Even after she rejected you. To top it all off, you didn't even talk about her to me. Which reminds me, may I know the reason for that, Hippi, sir?" She investigated him, grabbing his neck close with a scary voice.

Lenin *"Because that was a failure. A failed attempt at love for me!"*

Samyuktha *"Then, why didn't you- wait a minute! Why the fuck didn't you console me for my own past, Mr. Loser?"*

Lenin replied *"You were waiting to ask this question at the perfect time, right?"*

With that she softens her tone and words too *"I need to know you're clear about your own thoughts and emotions, that's why!"*

"I hate that my best friend who's been with me during tough times, who's taught me to be gentle, who will stand beside me even if I went crazy; I hate it when that best friend is bursting with tears in front of me. And I hated the thing that

made her feel like that, so much that I was paralyzed when she wanted to hold my hand. I am so-" he stops himself before he gets interrupted by another one of her tight slaps.

Her raised hands fall down to hold one of his cheeks, "*Even I hate the woman who rejected my Hippi.*"

Lenin blushed and replied "*Cut her some slack! She is still my ex.*"

Samyuktha winked "*Officially?*"

Lenin replied "*Well to her, yes. Not yet for me!*"

"*Ah of course. I know you man. You won't let go of your loved ones just like that. That's my sweet Hippi!*" Samyuktha finished her coffee and stole his too.

"*That's mine!*" Lenin pulled it back towards him.

"*No, that's mine!*" Samyuktha refused to give up the mug. Both of them started to fight for the coffee loudly, even forgetting that they were in a public place. "*No, I'm not giving it*" Lenin replied.

"*Lenin! We caught some eyes.*" Samyuktha became aware of her surroundings faster.

Both of them were seated on the very end of the first floor. Lenin turned to his left and saw people were watching them with interest for the Coffee cup finale.

After noticing the attention they've managed to grab, Lenin replied sarcastically, "*Eee sala cup namadhe*!"*

*"This cup is ours." - Translated from broken Hindi

After having that much-needed refreshing break, they both came down to set everything up for the ride to Coimbatore. Lenin moved first and opened the driver seat.

Samyuktha slowed down as she reached the car "*Hippi! Can I ask you something?*"

Lenin closes the door back and moves closer to her "*Of course, Sam. Go ahead!*"

"Do you like Parikshith as much as you like me?" she questioned.

"No, you are definitely on a higher level. But I do like him more when I am High! Why do you ask this now?" he shoots back.

"Then, why did a selfish creature jump into the lake to save you?" She asked him with curiosity.

"That's friendship! It's a boy's thing, you wouldn't understand. Come on, let's hurry up!" He moved her towards the car.

"Wait, that's what I am trying to tell you too. We women usually calculate the pros and cons for every situation around us. Meanwhile, men are prepared to die for each other. We will keep our minds alert and react to people depending on what they did to us, including both good and bad. So we normally don't give any particular reasons for rejecting someone." she said.

"What does that mean?" he asked with a hesitation.

Samyuktha *"Why do you, I mean men, have a mindset that a girl should promptly accept a proposal?"*

Lenin replied *"We don't!"*

Samyuktha *"Then, you should have accepted her rejection right?"*

Lenin slows down and thinks about it, *"I should have. But-"* his silence speaks of his apologies.

Samyuktha holds his hand and starts to explain briefly *"If she had just said No, then that would have been it. End of the line for both of you."*

Lenin put his head down muttering softly *"But Samyuktha, she said that she was committed."*

Samyuktha questioned *"Even if she didn't give you any explanation and simply said No, what would you have done?"*

Lenin sticks with this thought and he looks at her with hesitance, "*I would-*"

Samyuktha smiles back with a reply "*You should never disturb her post-proposal, if you are a decent human. You need to move on even with just the No. Let's imagine you took an important exam and failed. It doesn't mean you are unfit to attend any exams, right? Things that you deserve will come your way when the time is right for you.*"

Lenin smiled, nodded his head yes and asked "*You still use these exam metaphors?*"

Samyuktha laughs out loud and lays on the table facing him "*I never knew this side of you and how inexperienced you were in your relationships. It's fine because everybody makes mistakes at the first time. But remember this; even if everyone walks away, we are here for you Hippi. We are here to get you through everything!*"

Lenin breathes out a long sigh, falling back on his seat. He bursts out with tears, steadily covering his cheeks and chin, of both joy and regret. His face finally rests with a sigh and a sweet smile.

CHAPTER X

A Clear Picture

There is a new welcome, new life, new beginning complete refreshment started after brainstorming sessions filled trip, starting from the top;

A brilliant and caring girl step ahead college to purse her both love and professional life

One techie freak was standing in front of her girlfriend with a wedding ring to propose her

A very humbled and polite IT professional male getting prepared for kick-starting his work life

As usually the day begins with huge number of missed calls from his girl friend for cupid guy

One woman updating her curriculum vita in a matrimony site along with her family

In a crowded metro, Bold, brisk and beautiful lady along with her tools was in travel to present her business idea to a VC

Finally, the plot ends where it began from the start, Students were set up for Emotional Intelligence session presented by Lenin, and he connects his lap with a projector available inside the class, when everyone are watching he closely watches the door waiting for someone, eagerly, intentionally,

"*You want someone to approach for a start, Mr. Lenin?*" sarcastically questioned by Dr.Deepa.

"*No, Nope,*" he replied when they turn off the light and screen glows the light reflected by the white background in the projector

Door opens for last student, a tall, red dressed with black Hijab wore woman, Haya enters class seeking for permission "*May I?*"

Her accents provide a fresh energy for Lenin, her Hijab covered face resembled like a full moon in the star less night. Pretty much impressive and polite too

"*Yes, you should, otherwise presentation won't begin*" she replied with winkled pointing to Lenin

"*Ma'am, No*" he replied while whole class started to laugh

She sat in the middle row facing Lenin straight forward, just only for listening and listening sharply.

First slide beings with a smiley with quote "*I am committed!*"

"*Any guess?*" Lenin sparks out the first light

Everyone were rushed to answer "*It's a love quote*", Haya with swag reply "*Committed to been in emotional*"

Lenin's mind voice "*That's how you reply, I know you Idiot!*" But he replied" *Yes! Exactly*" he switches to next slide which indicates with a topic **Model for Emotion Regulation** and flow chart

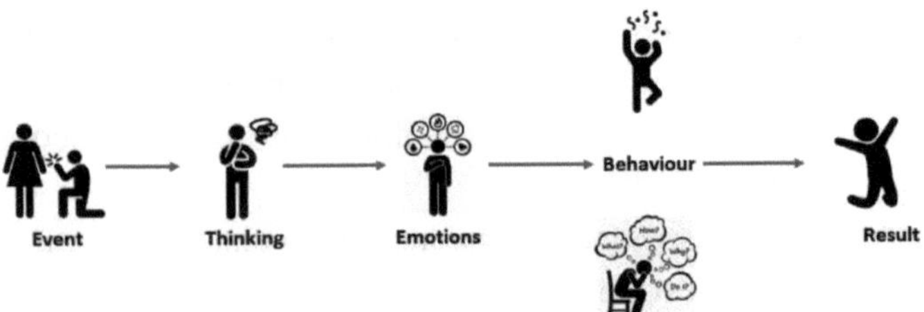

Model for Emotional Regulation

"I am going to present you a complete sketch of the Emotional Framework that can be triggered by a particular event let us discuss the successors for it" smiled Lenin and watches the audience reaction to check whether he is making it as right one to present

Event

"Emotions can be malleable that can be generated based on particular events" he said, one from the audience questioned *"like examples?"*

"Like... an individual attending an interview, Based on those individuals the interview events varies from their perspectives, here most of my targeted are teenagers I focused only on Love proposal that would familiar to everyone who were listening now" he pointed out

"So, what's your slide pointing out?" Dr.Deepa takes her chance to launch her query.

"Been an millennial, I mean one of Millennials, we were crossing many events, but I found this event, love relationship are one of usual and common for all, so I consider this as most eligible example to demonstrate emotional regulation framework" he justified his concerns

Dr. Deepa *"Okay, sounds logical. Move on!"*

Lenin continued *"Thank you Ma'am! Guys, If you are facing an event that triggers your emotions in a unexpected way, or most waited event that may turns to a stressful one which you may expecting to end as joyful, what will you do at that time?, any explanation!"*

"I will walk away!" Haya replied

Lenin mind voice *"That's what you do, always!"* But his words" *Any other answers!"*

"I will face it!" "I think to handle it in a better way" answers from each one of them made Lenin to felt that he is making an engaging session. "*Just a minute*" he heaved a deep time and tries to calm himself with a deep breath, shielding himself with emotions himself mention

"*You see a long breathe for 5 -10 seconds*" said Lenin, now he remembers how Samyuktha handled to control her tears when she revealed her past life.

"*This Long breathe controls your anger, stress or any emotions at current situation and make your emotions neutralize*" Lenin explains and felt about how does she felt to control her guilt

Everyone starts to practice his on-going therapy and he shouts out "*OKAY OKAY! Control your anger for god sake*"

Haya smiles all of a sudden.

Thinking

"*And, now the next phase is thinking! How does your emotions cause you to think if you got triggered when you in awful incident*" said Lenin and watches for their reaction.

"*Depending on the way you appraise an event, your emotions were triggered, you have ability to change the way by ending up in having a favorable emotions*" he explains.

One from audience "*Is it possible!*" "*Yes it is!*" He said and continues "*For example; what if a man, a known person for you, propose you for first time*"

She blushes and replies "*If he is good person I'll accept or else I'll reject*""*If he is good person and also if you reject him for some good intentions how will you feel?*" he said and looks Haya. Haya had figured the moment and startled. "*I feel guilt! And walk away from the place*" she replied.

"*There is best to way to overcome this stimulus, and that is reappraisal*" he explains and present from restart version of his life.

"*Reappraisal is looking in a different way how the opposite person thinking, For example, when I was in high we caught for using chits in exam, we were beaten up by strict teacher, By watching our punishment a girl in the first cries out with fear, meanwhile myself and my bench mates were enjoying the situation as a funny event, appraising an event can varies based on individuals. Can you understand?*" he explained and questioned.

One from the audience "*How do you connect reappraisal with this proposal event?*"

Lenin explains " *Imagine the man you rejected, had a one good female friend and If she consoled or else explain your situation to him from a woman point of view, and he recognized your silent, guilt, and Haya like your walk away from the place can be understood by the male. Now how would you feel for the rejection? Felt good right*" he questioned again

"*Yes, Very good master*" Amal replied with smile. A positive thought spark inside Haya.

Lenin laughs slightly and demonstrates "*By changing your thought process and you can prevent yourself from experiencing an unfavorable emotions*"

Emotions & Behavior

"*Reappraisal leads to emotions, apart from positive vibes. I'll explain you the other end, what if you could not avoid the event, you failed to reappraise it and you are experiencing an uncomfortable emotion. You can pause and redirect the thoughts to avoid manipulating your emotions.*"

Everyone shout out "*example.. Example?*"

" Yeah! I have an interesting one! Once you got cornered or blamed for a mistake that you didn't cause, how will your emotions trigger you, I mean till which incident?"

"May be, I turned upon rash driving" a male voice from the audience, *"This happened before, I broke the table glass after I had a fight with my mom & Dad"* another one from the audience end. *"See, you have triggered to hurt either yourself or your opposite humans. This is how our emotional Hijack leads us to a certain things!"*

"Do we can manage these emotions; I mean how can we overcome from this emotional Hijack?" a female voice raised.

"So Simple!" He passes on the next slide where it was a plain white slide with one text "**Hues**"

"Here I represented the Hues as your loveable ones; anybody can be your hues, just a chat with your favorable persons turn up your Emotion in a right way, or else I thinks a conversation with a right person at your con time will be best therapy session for you, some supportive words, a handshake, even a hug can calm you and get off from your emotional Hijack, change it as your modus operandi" he explains this context with the references to the incidents in Wayanad trip, how Samyuktha revealed her past, Hansi came through her hurdles, Yash emotional Balance, Michael found love treasure, Ayesha's acceptances and Parikshith priorities.

For Lenin he refereed Hues as Women, Woman who gave birth, friend who stood up in bad times, crush who thought some valuable things, he pin pointed Hues are women who are responsible for the colorful memories. He believes most of memorable moments were came up or built by a woman with a context to it he continues *"I am damn sure that most of your hues will be a woman, or else a woman will be present in your hues. How many of you accept my statement?"* questioned Lenin

After a 10 seconds gap, without turning their heads or looking for supportive response, everyone from the audience raised their hands to show off that Lenin delivered right context, Lenin knobs his heads down and takes a long breathe replies" *Thank you guys!*"

A warm polite female voice raised "*Chin up!*" Lenin understood this therapy, he smiles and look up for the voice generator, It was Haya, Haya Marium. Her tears reveal that she understood what Lenin felt and how did he came to understand her emotional Hijack.

"*Understand?*" He questions

"*Yes!*" Haya blushes with smile and tears

Result

At last, when he moves to next slide, **Result**; he continues by thinking about his much loved giggles, as they were with him in all kind emotions; happy, sad, anger, guilt, and many more. Even when situation turns upside down either they haven't let him go off or they didn't move aside from him. Likewise he closes his eyes and opens with wide shot, creating an illusion that they were seated among audience making fun for his presentations. With a smile and happy face he finishes his fruitful presentation.

"*That's it friends! Thank you for this patience and listening to me this much time;*

Hope you enjoyed my Presentation,"

"*Thank You! Thanks a lot!*"

I have coined the term "**Hues**" from the women who stay besides, tolerates, supports, believes and holds you even thought you expressed your negative shades.

Dedicated to all HUES :)

9 798885 213189

Printed by Libri Plureos GmbH in Hamburg,
Germany